The Valentine Box

TONI BLAKE

OLIVERHEBERBOOKS

To Jacqueline Daher

Your creative input and enthusiasm for my stories goes above and beyond.
I couldn't have done it without you.

Dear Reader,

When I started the first Box Book, The Wedding Box, it was an exercise in trying something new, taking an unusual concept and crafting a viable story around it. What it ended up delivering was catharsis, as it was the first book I'd written after the loss of both my parents. Since then, the Box Books have continued delivering that to me, in different ways. Without my planning it, they seem to draw in tidbits and memories from my youth, and in some cases even help me work through unresolved conflicts. Some readers have called these books "healing," and it turns out they're healing for the author, too.

I want to thank my dear friend, Jacqueline Daher, for all her help with this book. She has always read and supported my work, but with these last couple of books, she's been an indispensable part of my process, from brainstorming the story to giving me feedback on the finished product. Many of the "big ideas" in this particular story started with her, and I'm so grateful, not only for her help, but for her excitement and personal investment in the stories I tell. Writing a novel is a very solitary act, but it's nice to have a partner-in-crime.

My editor said, "Every page of The Valentine Box brims with warmth, poignancy, and the very meaning of love. A story sure to leave a lasting mark on every reader's heart." I hope that proves true for you! Thank you for reading my books!

Sincerely,
Toni Blake

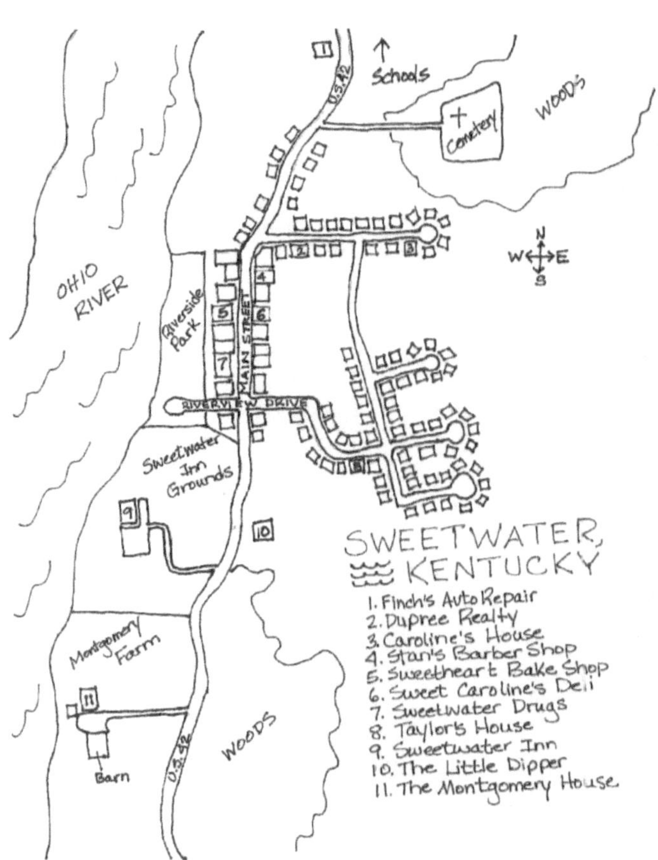

11
U.S. 42
Schools
WOODS
Cemetery
N
W E
S
OHIO RIVER
Riverside Park
MAIN STREET
2
3
4
5 6
7
RIVERVIEW DRIVE
8
Sweetwater Inn Grounds
9
10
Montgomery Farm
11
Barn
U.S. 42
WOODS
SWEETWATER, KENTUCKY
1. Finch's Auto Repair
2. Dupree Realty
3. Caroline's House
4. Stan's Barber Shop
5. Sweetheart Bake Shop
6. Sweet Caroline's Deli
7. Sweetwater Drugs
8. Taylor's House
9. Sweetwater Inn
10. The Little Dipper
11. The Montgomery House

4th GRADE

FEBRUARY 14

Taylor

"Ready?" Dad asks from behind the wheel of his beat-up Dodge pickup. His work truck, he calls it.

"No." Next to him, I keep my eyes straight ahead, on the stupid slush-covered road leading to the stupid school. I woke up hoping classes would be canceled today, but it didn't snow enough.

"Taylor," he says in that sensible, soothing way of his. I'm getting pretty tired of that, though. He promised me everything would be fine here, but he was wrong. Why did he have to take a stupid new job in stupid Sweetwater, Kentucky?

"I hate it here," I inform him.

"So you've said. A lot."

"I want to go back to Cincinnati." Where life was easy

1

and everyone was nice and I fit in. Where my red hair and freckles were just...red hair and freckles, and not some reason for other kids to treat me like a freak. We've only been here a week, but every day walking into Sweetwater Elementary feels like a brand new nightmare to navigate. I never knew I was so weird until the horrible kids in my class made it so clear to me.

"I know you do, sweet pea," he tells me. "And your mom and I are sorry you had to change schools in the middle of the year—we know that's not easy. But it was an opportunity we couldn't pass up." My dad is a carpenter—and a good one, everyone says—but he's been unemployed since the company he worked for went out of business right before Christmas. Now he's going to build homes at a development half an hour away. We live in a little house not nearly as nice as our old one in this dingy little town along the Ohio River. Every time I see that river, all I can think about is that it leads home, to Cincinnati. But I'm stuck *here*, in Sweetwater, where half the shops on Main Street are empty and all the kids are mean.

"Tay, look!" Dad says, leaning forward to peer out the windshield as he points. "A heart cloud."

I look, but struggle to make it out. "Sort of." Dad sees hearts everywhere—in the sky, in trees, in mud puddles, you name it. He claims to see a heart-shaped cloud about every other day. This one is a reach at best.

"Speaking of hearts," he says, "take a peek in the sack." He gestures toward the brown shopping bag sitting on the seat between us.

I've been aware of the bag the whole time we've been in

the truck. And I've heard my parents whispering about a "Valentine's Day surprise" for me. Is this it?

I reach inside and pull out...a heart-shaped box. It's about a foot wide, covered with beautiful carved designs, and the natural wood is a mix of colors from off-white to brownish to almost pink. On top is a narrow rectangular slot.

"It's really pretty," I say in awe. In fact, I'm not sure I've ever held anything so wonderful in my hands, the wood soft and smooth beneath my fingertips. "Did you make it?"

"Yep. It's cedar. It'll last forever, and it smells good."

I bend down to take a whiff. "Oh, it does."

"It's to collect your valentines in at school."

I'd noticed that Mom and I didn't decorate a shoebox for that this year. She's been busy unpacking and getting us settled, and I've been too depressed to care. I was okay with it being overlooked. "I'm not sure I'll get any," I confess.

At this, he leans over and gives my knee a reassuring pat. "Of course you will. You wrote them out for the other kids, didn't you?"

"Yeah," I say grudgingly. "Mom made me." Normally, it's an activity I enjoy, but this year, who cares? Mom picked up a box of them featuring cartoon cats and dogs. They say things like *Have a purr-fect Valentine's Day!* and *You're a pawsome friend!* and *Woof you be my Valentine?* I signed my name and addressed them to the list of kids the teacher sent home, but I'm almost embarrassed by it. I want to make friends, but so far I feel surrounded by enemies.

I study the box some more, running my fingers over the carved parts. "It looks like something you'd buy in a store, but better." I guess this is my way of telling him how talented I think he is. It's pretty amazing to me that my dad can make stuff like this. He's built a lot of shelves and other stuff for our family, too, but I think this is the coolest thing he's ever created. "How do you open it?" I ask, studying it.

"The top slides off. But you have to flip the little metal things on the bottom."

I turn it over. "Oh, I see." It's not obvious, which somehow adds to the beauty. It's like the box has a secret. I wish *I* had secrets. I wish I was mysterious and special enough to have secrets. But everything about me is plain to see. Curly red hair. Orange freckles. Glasses. It's confusing how I never knew everything about me was so unappealing until a few days ago, but now I feel the awkwardness just dripping from me.

When Dad pulls up in front of the one-story 1960s-style school, my stomach churns. I'd give anything to be back at home with Mom right now.

"Have a good day, sweet pea," Dad says with a smile. He's handsome, my dad. Dark-hair, loving eyes, a lean-but-rugged build. I wish I could make him understand how horrible it is in there, but his face is telling me to be brave. I want to be that: his brave girl, a daughter who makes him proud.

So I just say, "Okay," then struggle to gather up the gazillion things I'm toting inside: a Camp Snoopy lunchbox, a container of cookies Mom insisted we make last night, and my new valentine box.

But before I get out, I look over and say, "Thanks for the box, Daddy. I love it."

We're at the valentine-trading part of the day, so kids are up from their desks, moving around the room. Me, though, I'm sitting down, with the idea of dropping mine into boxes at recess time—if I can figure out who sits where, because I only know a few kids by name so far. One of them is Mitchell Dover.

So far, what I know about him is that he's constantly pushing his thick brown hair out of his eyes, and he's a terror on the dodgeball court—which I learned in gym class, cowering in a corner. He walks over to my desk and drops an envelope inside my special new box, eyeing it closely.

The teacher, a blonde woman named Mrs. Harmon who wears lots of sweaters that look alike, has stepped into the hall, where she's talking with the principal. I can hear them laughing. I haven't decided yet if she's an ally or another enemy. She *should* be an ally, but everything feels upside down here and she hasn't seemed very nice to me so far, for no reason I can figure out.

Mitchell Dover picks up one of the pink-frosted sugar cookies from the plastic container next to my box. "You make these?" he asks.

"Yes, with my mom."

Looking me squarely in the eye, he crushes the cookie into crumbs in his fist, letting them fall all over my desk, the valentine box, and the other cookies. It feels like he squeezed the life out of *me*, though. I'm stunned, gaping at him, wondering why he just destroyed something I worked hard on. It stings, and a heavy lump grows in my throat.

That's when he pulls a thick, black marker from his pants pocket, yanks off the cap, and scribbles all over the top of my heart-shaped cedar box. I yank the box away, hugging it to my chest as I yell, "Stop it!"

"*Stop it*," he mimics me in a babyish voice, then laughs.

Glancing down, I see that the wet ink has stained my new top, white and speckled with red hearts. It's ruined. My eyes hurt and my throat burns and I'm trying desperately to hold back tears, but they're rolling thick and heavy down my hot cheeks anyway.

"Are ya gonna cry, little baby? *Wah, wah.* Cry, little baby, cry."

Mitchell Dover laughs and points at me, drawing me to the attention of anyone who hasn't yet tuned in. Some kids laugh along with him while others just stare. But more are laughing than not and no one is coming to my rescue. Not that it would help now anyway. My top is destroyed, and so is the beautiful box my father made for me.

Directly to my right sits another of the few kids I know by name so far, Luke Montgomery. Sandy-haired and lanky, I've already figured out he's popular, and sporty. Kids talk about him quarterbacking peewee football and I heard him telling his friends about the baseball glove he got for Christmas. His father is our new family doctor, so I guess he's rich. From the corner of my eye I see him watching me.

Even as Mitchell Dover retreats across the room, all smug and proud of his hatefulness, even as other kids get back to the business of valentines, the good-looking little boy in the row of desks next to mine keeps watching me and it only embarrasses me all the more. Doesn't he have anything better to do? Doesn't he need to hand out valentines?

Luke

Mitchell's a jerk. What did that girl ever do to him? I feel sorry for her, and there's a part of me that thinks I should step in to help her in some way, but another part of me knows that would only make me the next target.

Still, she keeps crying. Crying and crying. Her shirt's all messed up, and so is the cool box she brought in.

"Listen," I lean over to say, trying to be quick about it, "don't bother telling Mrs. Harmon. She's Mitchell's step-mom. He won't get in trouble—she'll just turn it back on you some way."

She looks up at me through her tear-stained glasses, but says nothing, maybe because I've just made her situation even worse.

"Hi, Luke."

I flinch, then look up to see Jasmine Dupree drop a white envelope in the shoebox my mom covered in red wrapping paper last night. "Hi, Jasmine."

"You playing little league this spring?"

I just nod. She's been in my grade since kindergarten, but lately she won't leave me alone. She and I were elected to represent the fourth grade at the fall festival in October, so I had to walk with her across the stage, and she kept leaning on me. She has long, blonde hair, almost to her waist, curled under at the ends.

"So is my big brother," she goes on, "so I'll be at your games."

"Okay."

"Happy Valentine's Day," she says.

"Thanks." What I really mean, though, is: *Go away*. She just bugs me.

"All right, everyone, it's time for recess," Mrs. Harmon says, stepping back in the room. If she's noticed the crying girl with black ink all over her top, it doesn't show. "Finish up with your valentines, then find your coats and line up next to the door."

I quickly circle past Jasmine to connect with my buddy, TJ, ready to get up a game of basketball as soon as we hit the playground. But then I see Mrs. Harmon zero in on the new girl, walking over and bending down to talk with her. I hope the girl takes my advice—Mitchell can get away with anything in this class and he knows it. In fact, he's watching the whole thing and looking cocky as ever. It kinda makes my skin itch.

A minute later, the whole class is in line, zipping up coats and pulling on hats and gloves—all except the new girl. And that's when Mrs. Harmon announces, "Someone has defaced Taylor's box and shirt, but she's refused to tell me who, apparently afraid of retribution. Would the culprit like to come forward and take responsibility, or does the whole class have to be punished?"

This brings about a lot of moaning and groaning, but no confession from her stepkid.

"All right then," she says. "I'll use recess to think about how we're going to deal with this situation." Then she switches her gaze back to the girl. "Though this would be a lot easier if you'd just tell me who did it."

Even now, it gets turned back on her, like she's done something wrong. Talk about a no-win situation.

Mrs. Harmon looks irritated, and there's a part of me tempted to just come forward and say what I saw. But every time anyone tells on Mitchell, nothing happens besides getting on her bad side.

"All right, out you go," she says, shooing the whole class. "Taylor, you may stay here and collect yourself."

As we reach the door and exit onto the playground, I hear Mitchell Dover say to a group of kids, "That girl's so stupid. Like a little mouse, afraid of everything. Guess I can do whatever I want to her. I *rule* this school."

Without planning it, I step into his path and he bumps up against me. I don't move away as we make eye contact, and he warns, "Watch it."

"She didn't speak up," I explain, "because I told her you hide behind your new mommy's skirt."

I watch his pale face turn beet red. "You take that back, Montgomery."

"Who's gonna make me?"

But instead of giving him time to answer, I follow the gut instinct to shove him to the ground.

Taylor

As I sit down to dinner with my parents, they're both outraged on my behalf, and Dad wants to go to the school and demand a meeting with the teacher. I'm begging him not to, explaining it can only make things worse, and Mom is saying, "But we can't just let things like this go unchecked or they'll keep happening."

"I don't think that boy will bother me again," I inform them quietly.

"Why's that?" Mom asks.

"Another boy beat him up at recess. The same one who was a little bit nice to me and told me about the teacher being that boy's stepmom."

At this, my parents' eyes get even bigger, and I can tell they're not sure how to respond. And they don't have to. I already know fighting is bad, but I also know it's the nicest thing anyone's done for me since I set foot in this town.

Of course, I have no guarantee that's what the fight was about—all I know is that both boys were hauled back in by their shirt collars with bloody noses and torn clothes. But as they stood outside the classroom getting yelled at by the principal, Luke Montgomery looked in through the doorway at me and our eyes met across the room. Until the principal yelled at him *louder*, for not listening, and he turned away.

Now my gaze lifts to the cedar box sitting on our kitchen counter. "I'm so mad about the box," I say, the very sight of it nearly pushing me to tears all over again. It's been a rough day. "I know you worked hard on it, Daddy, and I loved it."

He reaches out to squeeze my hand, currently clenched stressfully-tight around a fork. "We can fix it, sweet pea."

I blink, stunned, loosening my grip. "We can?"

He nods. "A little primer and paint'll work wonders. It won't look exactly the same, but it'll still be nice, just in a different way. You can pick out whatever color you want."

I nod, relieved and liking the idea. "Good. I'm gonna keep it forever."

After dinner, as I sit doing homework at the table, I see Mom eyeing me from where she's working at the kitchen sink. She has red hair, too—but it's prettier, straighter, and darker than mine, falling just to her shoulders. All red hair is definitely not created equal.

Finally she asks, perhaps cautiously, "Do you want to open the box and go through your valentines?"

All things considered, I really don't. But she adds, "It'll cheer you up."

Mostly, it doesn't. It's just a bunch of silly little cards, all signed by people I don't know—and those are the good ones. The bad ones are the few left *un*signed, on which kids actually took the time to write out mean messages.

You're ugly.

You walk funny.

You look weird.

It's hard to keep going, but for some reason I do. Maybe there's one I'm specifically waiting to find.

And just when I start to think maybe there isn't one from him, I open the last envelope in the bottom of the scribbled-on box and there it is.

To Taylor Mulvaney. From Luke Montgomery.

That's all it says, in tidy blue ink.

Looks like his mother bought him the very same package of valentines as mine. I study a familiar cartoon dog with a circle around one eye and the words up above: *Woof you be my valentine?*

I know it's random, just the card in his hand when he reached my name on the list, but I still can't help thinking: *Maybe I woof.*

8th Grade

FEBRUARY 14

Taylor

Ah, another Valentine's Day. Thank God this is the last year we'll be forced to trade cards—as middle schoolers, we're already too old for it. Now the valentines come with subtext and unanswered questions.

"Does that mean he likes me, in *that* way?"

"I thought she hated me, but that's a really cute card, so maybe I'm wrong?"

"Maybe that boy isn't as mean as I thought?"

My friend, Caroline Loder, has in fact, turned from the desk in front of mine to ask those very questions all within the past two minutes.

We became friends in speech therapy in fifth grade. Both

of us had lisps and were taken out of class to meet with a special teacher in the library every other Tuesday. Caroline was born in Sweetwater, but has been just as much of an outcast as me. Her lisp was more pronounced than mine, and she's a few sizes bigger than most of the girls, wearing hand-me-downs from older siblings that don't fit her body well. So never mind what being singled out for speech therapy did to our already incredibly-low social standing—we bonded. We don't have much in common other than trying to keep a low profile and not get beat up, but that's enough.

"Have you looked at yours yet? Why aren't you looking at yours?" Caroline spins to ask me.

"I'm gonna wait until later, do it privately."

Sometimes I still get anonymous mean cards—even though Mitchell Dover moved away, thank God. But the main reason I'm waiting is because the valentine box has become even more meaningful to me this past year.

Last June, my dad fell three stories from a house he was working on and severed his spinal cord. He died instantly. A doctor explained to me about damage to some nerve that controls breathing, but all I really heard was that my father was gone in a heartbeat.

Now my mom waits tables at the Sweetheart Diner, an old restaurant on Main Street that's struggling to survive, like most of the businesses around here—and now *I'm* the one who see hearts everywhere I go. It's been a tough year for us both.

After the original defacing of the valentine box, Dad and I painted it white and, to my surprise, that made it even prettier. I've continued to collect my cards in it every year, but after today, I'll have to find other uses for it.

And in the spirit of doing things privately, I use this moment to reach in my backpack and sneakily pass Caroline a small stack of heart-shaped cookies in a cellophane bag. "Put these away and don't eat them until later," I instruct her.

Her eyes light up at the sight, but then she catches on, tucking them discreetly in her book bag. "Thanks," she whispers. "You know I love your cookies."

Baking cookies, cakes, and pies with my mom has become a big thing in my life—it's something we love doing together. Or we *did* anyway. She works so much now that she's exhausted by the time she gets home, so I've mostly been baking on my own lately. But I've never brought any to share with classmates other than Caroline since that scarring fourth grade incident. Fool me once and all that. I've learned to keep my guard up. I still don't fit in, but I've slowly found ways to navigate this stupid school.

"Hey."

I look up at the low, clipped greeting from Luke Montgomery as he slides into the desk next to mine in our alphabetically-designated homeroom.

"Hey," I say back.

All these years later, we've never discussed that fight between him and Mitchell, but we've been quietly friendly ever since. We don't hang out, of course—popular, athletic boys like him congregate with their own kind—but he's always nice to me. He sits next to me in homeroom, same as in elementary school, and sometimes he asks me for a pencil or ink pen, with a *yeah-forgot-again-sorry* grin I've grown used to. I just make sure I have an extra now. Most of the other jocks and cheerleaders treat me like I don't exist, but not Luke.

"Oh—here," he says in that same low voice as he leans over to drop a small envelope into the slot on the valentine box.

I can't hold in a probably-too-bashful smile. "Thanks."

Then he hands one to Caroline and she responds, "Thank you, Luke," in a whispery way that sounds like she's being wooed. I love the girl, but there are reasons we're not in the cool kids' club.

He sounds completely embarrassed and awkward as he stands up and says, eyes averted from us, "Better hand these out before the bell." Then he pulls up short. "Oh, almost forgot." He reaches in his backpack and extracts a small red-wrapped shoebox that's seen better days and plops it on his desk, muttering, "Man, I can't wait to have this tradition over with."

"You and me both," I murmur, and he tosses me a quick, pleasant glance before heading to the other side of the room, a stack of mini-envelopes in his hand.

Caroline rips into the one Luke just handed her and reads it out loud. "You're so cool, valentine." I peek over her shoulder to see a cartoon polar bear standing on a chunk of ice. "Do you think he really thinks I'm cool?" she asks.

I just sigh. "Sorry, but...probably not, Care. No one thinks *either* of us is cool. My mother says that will change when we get older, though, or that it quits mattering very much, or something."

"Hope so," she says on a sigh of her own.

Valentines are only exchanged in homeroom, thank goodness. On the way to my first period class, I stash the box in my locker, and I pick it up again before last period, since my locker is in the opposite direction as the school buses. I'm a little surprised to see no one else toting a box of valentines—maybe they're all crammed into book bags or they were cardboard ones ditched in the nearest trash can after the cards were removed. The box sits on the corner of my desk as we take a quiz.

Algebra I is kind of a Who's Who of Sweetwater Middle School. On one side of the room sits Jasmine Dupree and some of the other cheerleaders, all gorgeous and confident and domineering. Toward the middle are Luke and his friends, TJ and Billy—the cool ballplayer contingent. Luke is the only friendly one, but the other two at least seem like decent guys. Mix in a couple of brainiacs, a budding track star, and some middle-of-the-roaders—not popular but not nerds—and that leaves Caroline and me, over by the windows, trying to keep our usual low profile.

Just before the final bell dismisses us for the day, Mr. Cortez steps out of the classroom, ready to play hall monitor. There was some roughhousing in the halls last week, so the teachers have been told to stay on guard.

Almost as soon as he's out of sight, I spot Jasmine Dupree eyeing me from across the room. She's become a problem the last few months. Until this year, the popular girls just ignored me, but Jasmine has started looking for reasons to give Caroline and me a hard time lately.

Same as the first day I arrived in Sweetwater, I have no idea why certain kids get so much pleasure from terrorizing others. Especially people like Jasmine. Her father's a lawyer and her mother a successful realtor, she's gorgeous and dresses like a fashion model, she's a cheerleader, and all the cute boys like her—what more does she want from middle school? When she gets up and crosses the room toward me, I have a feeling I'm about to find out.

My desk is the first in the row and she comes to stand right in front of me. "Wow, look at red's fancy valentine box," she says loudly enough to get the entire class's attention. Life was easier when she didn't notice me or the heart-shaped box I've brought to school on this day every year since I moved here.

"She must be *super* excited about Valentine's Day," she goes on, switching her gaze back and forth between her friends across the room and the heart-shaped box. "Must think she's getting lots of *passionate* valentines from all the boys." She stops to let out a deep laugh, but her eyes are vicious. "I bet she goes home and reads them, thinking they're for real. Can't you just see her, blushing and fantasizing, thinking they really like her? I wonder who she has the biggest crush on."

Now her eyes roam the boys in the room. "Maybe it's Luke," she says, her eyes landing on him. "I bet she thinks he's *soooo* cute." My chest aches as my face burns with embarrassment, surely turning bright red.

"Or maybe it's TJ. He's all tall, dark, and handsome. Or maybe she's hot for Billy. Maybe she just swoons every time he shoots a three-pointer." Another sickening laugh leaves her, and that's when she adds, "Or maybe she sends fake valentines to herself, so she can pretend she has a love life. Let's look and see!"

At that precise moment, the bell rings and she scoops up the wooden heart box from my desk to dart out of the room into an instantly crowded hallway. Her friends all laugh and follow—as Luke says, "Don't worry, Taylor—I'll go after her."

He's holding a notebook in his hand, using it to gesture toward the door Jasmine just exited, and on the back cover, I notice a discoloration of some kind—shaped like a heart. I really do see them everywhere now—at least once a week, often more.

Sometimes I wonder if I'm imagining them, just craving some way to believe my father's still with me. But Geneva, my mother's waitress friend at the diner, says that whatever my heart tells me is true. And what my heart's telling me right now is that this is from my dad. And that he's sending me one of the same messages, or wishes, he always had for me: he wants me to be brave. He doesn't want me to go through life being walked on. So even as tempting as it is to let Luke Montgomery handle this, I hear myself answer, "No, I need to do this myself."

Of course, as I step out into the hall, catching a glimpse of Jasmine and her crew in the distance heading toward the gym, I have no idea what it is I'm going to do, and I'm terrified something bad is going to happen to my precious box. I struggle through the crowd, afraid I'll lose sight of her and my box will disappear.

As I fight my way down the hall, I realize how much more sense it would have made to let Luke do it—he offered, and wouldn't it just gall Jasmine for him to be my knight in shining armor? But as I spot Jasmine and company pushing their way through the gym door, I remember that heart I saw, and what I felt in my gut: I'm sick and tired of this horrible girl persecuting me and my friend.

I just hope I don't regret whatever's about to happen.

When I burst through the gym door, I see kids spread out, making posters—*Go Tigers!* and *Tigers Gonna Roar!*—and taping twisted crepe paper to the orange-and-white painted concrete walls. There's a pep rally tomorrow.

I've made quite an entrance, so every gaze turns my way.

I, on the other hand, only have eyes for my valentine box, tucked under Jasmine's arm. She appears as surprised to see me as I am to be here—even more so as I barrel straight toward her. I try to look as mean as her, demanding, "Give me my box."

But she still seems completely in control. "Aw, afraid I'll read all your valentines?" she asks in her awful, ridiculing way.

"Give it back."

She raises her eyebrows, smug as ever. "Or what?"

Okay, mean isn't working. Mean is something she understands and excels at.

So maybe I need to take my game to a new level and go with...crazy. I need to act scary-crazy. Or...maybe it's for real —I've been driven to this. I take a step closer and say in my most venomous voice, "You don't wanna find out."

But Jasmine only laughs. "Is that so?"

Don't give up, though. Go at it harder. "Wanna try me?"

"Are you gonna beat me up, red?"

And that's when I commit to full-on nut-job crazy, speaking in a low, quiet, threatening voice I didn't even know I possessed. "I'm not sure yet. I'll have to give it some thought. Figure out exactly the best way to hurt you, and when."

I'm not a violent person—I can barely kill a housefly—but this finally produces a chink in Jasmine's smug armor. She looks less confident, thrown off by the fact that I might just be dangerous and insane. So I keep going. "I hope having to wonder when it will happen, having to look over your shoulder every second of your stupid, pompous life will be worth it. Is it? Worth it?"

Jasmine continues to stare me down, but I think she's afraid now and doesn't know what to do.

Courtney Jones, one of her cheerleader buddies, says, "Jasmine, her father made that box and he's dead. Why don't you just give it back?"

"Fine, whatever," Jasmine mutters. "It's stupid anyway." Then she tosses it in my general direction—and I barely catch it just before it crashes to the floor.

With my heart beating a mile a minute—in both relief and fear—I turn and exit the gym.

I nearly run head-on into Luke Montgomery, pulling up short just before we collide. He's holding out my book bag. "You forgot this."

I blink repeatedly, stunned and a little horrified as I take it from him. "Thanks." Then I nibble my lower lip, struggling to make eye contact. "Did you...see what just happened? In the gym?" *Please say no. I don't want you to think I'm a crazy psycho killer.*

"Yeah," he says.

And I wish desperately for the tile floor beneath me to open up and swallow me whole.

Luke

"You were scary," I tell her. "And awesome."

I watch her green eyes go wide behind her glasses. "Awesome?"

I nod, impressed. "She's not an easy person to scare, but I think you did it."

"I'm not really crazy," she tells me, shaking her head vigorously.

"I know," I assure her on a light laugh. "But you did what you had to, and it was hella cool."

As she gives her head a cute tilt, I get a better look at her. I've gone to school with her for years, and we've always been friendly enough, but we're not usually standing face to face like this. People make fun of her freckles, but I kinda like 'em.

"Thanks," she says, seeming a little bashful. Then she scrunches up her nose. "I don't know why she's so mean when she already has everything she could possibly want."

I just shake my head, equally at a loss.

"How come you hang around with her?" she asks me then.

I didn't see that coming and I'm not sure how to answer. "I don't, exactly," I claim. It's true. "She's just part of my friend group."

"Not a very nice one." Her mood has gone a little darker

again, and I guess I can't blame her. I've never been bullied, but I'm sure it sucks.

And I've never *been* a bully—but maybe I've never done much to stop it, either. Other than that time I beat up Mitchell Dover in the fourth grade. I got in so much trouble with my dad for that—I kinda gotta walk the straight and narrow with him. Guess maybe I feel like I'm walking a thin line *most* of the time, in lots of ways.

"Hey, you mad at me?" I ask her.

"No. I just don't like your *friend*." She puts the last word in air quotes.

"I hear ya. She's a jerk. The cheerleaders and ballplayers just get shoved together a lot." It sounds weak even as it leaves me, but that's true, too. And Jasmine never acts like this at parties or on the away game bus. Though I'm sure Taylor doesn't want to hear me explain that she actually has a normal side.

"I get it," Taylor answers quietly. And if I'm honest with myself, the way she says it slugs me in the gut a little. Like what she's really saying is: *I get that even though you're nice to me, you're still more like her.*

And I kinda want to take up for myself, explain some more, but I'm not sure she's wrong.

"Thanks for bringing my bag," she tells me, still looking disheartened, and I'm not sure if that's about what happened with Jasmine or if it's somehow about me. But my dad always tells me I'm too full of myself, so maybe this proves it.

"Sure," I say, watching as she strides toward the row of windowed doors leading outside.

That's when she looks out, muttering, "Well, this is just *great*," and her eyes fall dejectedly shut.

"What's wrong?" I step over and glance out myself to see a row of yellow school buses pulling away from the curb outside in a single-file line.

"Your *friend*," she says with more air quotes, "made me miss my bus."

"She's still not my friend," I insist.

At this, Taylor lets her eyes go comically wide as she replies, "Okie dokey—whatever you say. Wink, wink." She ends with an exaggerated wink that makes me laugh.

And then she laughs, too.

But that's when I remember she has a problem—one I can actually help with. "My brother Aaron is picking me up. He can take you home."

Taylor

Talk about a day that turned out differently than expected. First I get into a near-scuffle with Jasmine over my heart box, and now I'm clutching the box in one arm and my book bag in the other as I climb into Luke's brother's car. It's a late-model sedan, nicer than any car my family's ever owned. He's a senior at the high school that sits a parking lot away from the middle school.

I'm ridiculously nervous and instantly worried I'll do something wrong, socially or otherwise.

"This is Taylor—she needs a ride home," Luke explains. He's in the backseat, having insisted I sit in front. I'd feel more comfortable if our positions were reversed, though.

"Cool. Where do you live?" I guess I was worried the brother would size me up, see me as so many in Sweetwater do—the weird girl with the red hair and freckles. So I'm actually grateful when he doesn't bother to look at me even while sounding okay with the situation.

"On Riverview, just off Main." I've always felt cheated that our end of Riverview has no river view—in fact, *most* of Riverview has no view—and it's a far nicer name than the street delivers. Truthfully, I'm even a little embarrassed to even say it, knowing they live in a large, picturesque Victorian home on a horse farm that lines the river for a mile or more. Sporting gingerbread trim and a large, wraparound porch, it's flanked by rows of the white split-rail fencing common to Kentucky horse country.

"Cool," he says again, emotionless. "Just give me directions when we get into town."

The ride is mostly silent, other than the radio, until Luke's brother says to me, "Cool box."

He's a guy of few words, and most of them seem to be *cool*.

"Thanks. My dad made it," I tell him. I continue to feel sheepish, suddenly immersed in the world of the Montgomery family, but I'm pleased he admired the box.

Luke's brother flips around on the radio, and when he hits a song I recognize but have never actually heard playing randomly anywhere, I say, "Oh, I know this song. It's a great song."

Though I immediately regret blurting it out. I intended to stay quiet unless spoken to—the best way to navigate social situations one is thrust into because there's less opportunity for people to think you're weird. So it's a relief when Luke actually sounds interested, asking, "Oh yeah?"

And I explain. "It's called 'Lady in Red.' My mom and dad danced to it at their high school homecoming dance. And then again at their wedding. And they dance to it every year on their anniversary. Or, I mean, they did. Until..."

"Until what?" the brother asks casually.

See, this is why I stay quiet. Especially lately. Sometimes I say things I don't mean to. And now I'm stuck. "He died last year."

"Oh. Shit." It's the first time Luke's brother has glanced my way and I've made his eyes go wide with shock.

"It's all right," I rush to tell him.

But now he looks even *more* taken aback. "It is?"

"Well, not really," I confess. "I mean, he's dead and it's awful. I just didn't mean to make anyone uncomfortable. Sorry." I end on a tired sigh, staring down at the knees of my blue jeans, wishing I'd found some other way home.

That's when a hand closes over my shoulder, and I turn to find Luke's face closer to mine than it's ever been. "Hey, nothing to be sorry for." But then his touch is gone, and his face, too, as he says, "Turn it up."

Luke's brother increases the volume and the song plays. Watching my parents dance to it year after year growing up... well, I just heard their love in it somehow. But hearing the song now, in the awkwardness of Luke's brother's car, I realize it's a soulfully, desperately, almost painfully romantic song. And somehow even *that* embarrasses me, on the inside, as it hits me I'm not a girl any guy is ever going to feel that way about.

My internal strife eases only when the song ends and Luke's brother amuses me by saying, "Cool tune."

My sheepishness returns, however, as the car glides up Main, where even more of the shops are closed than when we first moved here, and I direct Luke's brother to our bland little house a few blocks away, its faded white siding and cracked driveway suddenly looking more faded and cracked to me than ever. "This one," I say, pointing, and he stops the car. "Thanks for the ride."

As I get out and start up the driveway, feeling small inside to have Luke see where I live as he vacates the back-seat to move up front, he calls behind me. "Hey, Taylor."

I stop, look over my shoulder.

"Happy Valentine's Day."

I hope I'm not blushing as I say, "Happy Valentine's Day, Luke."

As the classy car pulls away, I think about their big, beautiful home with the river in the backyard. It's the prettiest house in town. As I dig out my key and let myself in, I miss my dad. Mom is at work and won't be home until after nine. Life wasn't supposed to be like this, for either of us.

I do my homework, then heat up leftover meatloaf, making some instant mac and cheese to go with it. After I clear my dishes from the table, I sit back down and take the lid off the valentine box. My heart beats a little faster with a secret wish that maybe there'll be something noteworthy about the one from Luke.

But it's only his name, same as every year. On the other side: *You're sweet, valentine,* with a picture of a smiling cupcake.

Oh no, I've just become what Jasmine accused me of—a girl who fantasizes the popular boy likes her! Ugh. And worse yet, do I actually have a crush on Luke Montgomery?

I think longingly back to that first valentine I ever received from him. *Woof you be my valentine?*

Oh, I definitely woof, Luke. I definitely woof.

Only that can never be. *I could never fit into your world, and you'll never see me the way I wish you would.*

12th grade

Taylor

I sit in homeroom making notes in a three-ring binder about my schedule for the coming week.

I need to study for a world history test on Friday, and there are no words to express how much I dread my book report on Lord of the Flies in lit class. It's not that I don't write a great report; it's that I have to deliver it aloud to the whole class.

There's a *Tiger Tribune* meeting tomorrow after school—I'm the business manager for the school newspaper, which basically means I do all the parts besides writing and editing it. And back in the fall when kids were out sick with the flu, I did that, too.

I started a baking club, and on Thursday after school,

seven of us will be whipping up fruit tarts in the family sciences classroom, the one place in this building where I feel confident and comfortable. Not that I'm any expert on family, having such a tiny one—basically now just my mom and my aunt Helen, who lives an hour away—but baking has remained my passion. I might not know how to talk to boys, but I can make a pineapple upside down cake like nobody's business. And I might not be very handy with a makeup brush, but pass me a whisk or a rolling pin and I'm in my element.

So I guess you could say I've...found my way here over time. I still don't have many friends, but I've immersed myself in other things.

As more kids enter the classroom, I glance up, keeping an eye out for Luke. One of the best things about my time at Sweetwater High has been my friendship with him. Not that it's really changed all that much. We're homeroom buddies. We say hi when we pass in the hall. He always has a smile for me, and he's always kind.

But do we hang out? No. But did I ever expect that? Also no. We're from two different worlds, he and I. And I'd never feel comfortable in his.

As for my crush on him? It's still there. But it's just a crush. Just an awareness that he keeps getting cuter with age. Just a tingling of my skin whenever he's near. Just a wish for something that can never be.

In four months we graduate. He's bound for the University of Kentucky in Lexington with a lot of his friends. It's only ninety minutes away, but it might as well be on another planet. I'll still be stuck in this ailing little town, driving to a community college half an hour down I-71, going on grants and scholarships. Thank God for those or I wouldn't be going at all.

As I underline: *Remind Tiger staff to sell sweetheart wishes*, Luke slides into the desk behind me with a bit of a jolt. I turn to face him with a teasing grin. "Well, good morning to you, too."

Yet I don't get anything even close to a smile in return. It's more of a grimace, coming through sullen eyes. "Morning."

In the eight years I've known Luke Montgomery, I've never seen him like this. So I'm thrown, and wondering if I should just turn back around and leave him alone—but instead, I cautiously venture, "What's the word of the day?"

It's a thing that started between us last year—because apparently Dr. Montgomery uses a lot of technical medical words that amuse Luke. Like *phalanges* for *fingers*, or *hallux* for *big toe*. So Luke makes conversation by giving me the "word of the day." And it extended from medical language into more everyday stuff when he once spun toward me and said, "Word of the day—chicanery. What my father accused me of being involved in last weekend."

"Were you?" I asked.

He gave me a sneaky grin, holding up his index finger and thumb, close together. It made something in chest sizzle.

Now, he goes silent and stone-faced, eyes downcast, and I'm sorry I asked—until he answers, "*Angry*. The word of the day is *angry*."

I take a deep breath, gathering the courage to quietly pry. "What's wrong?"

In response, he blows out a humongous sigh. "We're moving."

At this, my eyes bolt open wide. *"What? Where?"*

It's the first time his gaze has lifted to meet mine and in it I see utter despair. "Cincinnati. My dad accepted a job at a big practice there."

I draw back slightly, dumbfounded. His father is my doctor; he's *everyone's* doctor in Sweetwater. "You're kidding."

"Nope. Says he wants to try something besides small town medicine. Apparently it's been in the works a while, but no one bothered to tell me. The plan was to wait until after I graduated, but some opportunity came along that he claims he can't pass up."

"Okay, wait. This is happening *before* we graduate?" I ask, confused.

"Yup. Leaving in two weeks."

"Two weeks?" I probably look as upset as he feels, because I am. The one and only thing I've dreaded about graduation was no longer seeing Luke. And finding out it's going to happen even sooner—like in the blink of an eye!—is crushing.

He nods, then takes a deep breath and blows it back out, clearly trying to keep hold of his emotions. But they're still pulsating out of him and onto me. "I can't graduate with the people I've gone to school with for twelve years. Hell, I can't even finish the basketball season. TJ's mom offered to let me live with them the rest of the school year, but Dad said no. And Mom wanted to stay here, in the house, her and me, until graduation, but he nixed that, too. He's all 'family stays together,'" Luke goes on, mimicking a deep, gruff voice for that part. "As if he's ever given a shit about me. He sure doesn't give a shit about what *matters* to me, I know that much."

It's hard to hide how shattered I am by this news—from him, and from me. It's like a reckoning inside me.

In summers, I've missed seeing him, living for days on a chance meeting at the gas station or the Sweetwater Diner. (Mom still waits tables there and her boss, Walt, sometimes pays me to bake pies and cakes.) But I also knew I'd see him again come August, almost every day. And this year, I've known graduation was coming, but it's felt far away, like a loss somewhere out in the distance. Learning that in two weeks I'll probably never see Luke Montgomery again feels like the end of the world as I know it.

I never realized. How deep my crush ran. Or that...maybe it's more of an attachment than a crush. More of a...caring. More of an ache deep inside me—eased by our every-morning conversations. And if there are suddenly no more of those... it's gotten difficult to breathe.

"This is...awful," I murmur, trying to sound like I feel as bad for him as I actually do for myself.

Fortunately, he's so wrapped up in his own problems that he doesn't notice my distress. "They're putting the farm up for sale. They're selling our horses. Man, I *love* those horses."

A big, pretty barn sits near the Montgomery house, home to half a dozen horses. Sometimes in summer, I think of excuses to ask Mom to drive past with the hope of catching a glimpse of Luke on horseback from the road. Once, I did. He looked majestic and rugged, like a cowboy. And so close in one sense, but in another, so very far away.

"I'm really sorry, Luke," I say. "I remember what it's like to be yanked away from someplace where you're happy, where you belong. It's the worst."

He gives his head a slight tilt, obviously having not made that connection. "That's right—you were once the new kid way back when, weren't you?"

"From Cincinnati, too," I remind him with a nod. "I loved my school there. Leaving was horrible, and coming here was worse than I could have imagined."

His expression tells me he's not forgotten what it was like for me then, and sometimes still is. "I'm sorry you've had such a rough time here."

Yet I just head-shake it away—this is about *me* empathizing with *him*. "It's hard to be uprooted. And I can see now that my parents didn't really have a choice. But the fact that you *could* stay and your dad won't let you..." I stop, sigh. "It's not fair."

As I talk, I'm aware of sandy hair that could use a trim—though the unkempt look works on him, in the same way it does a ski bum or surfer boy. Even in February, he's like the outdoors personified. I gaze into blue eyes that seem bluer today than they ever have before—and I can't believe that in just two short weeks I'll never get to look into them again. I take in broad shoulders, a strong jaw, the masculine hands resting in front of him on the desk—all these little pieces of male beauty that are about to be ripped away from me.

When I raise my glance back from his hands to his face, he's looking directly at me. I didn't expect that. His gaze is electric. "Know what, Taylor? I think you're the nicest girl in this whole school."

I blink at the unexpected compliment. "I am?"

He nods. "Since you haven't always had the easiest time of it here, this is selfish of me, but...I'm glad you came to Sweetwater."

Am I glad, too? It's impossible to even conceive of who I would be if we hadn't moved when I was a kid. Maybe I'd be well-adjusted and confident. And maybe...my father would still be alive. So no, I can't say I'm glad I came, too. But I *can* dare to tell him, "You've been one of the few bright spots for me in this dingy little town."

Except...holy crap. That was *big*. I've told him he stands out. In my existence. That I've noticed. That he's more than just my homeroom buddy. Ugh.

I wait for a reaction, but that's when the bell rings, the last few kids slide into their desks, and Miss Curtis starts calling roll. So I turn back to face frontward, and am glad for the timing as my face heats to what is surely a vivid sunburn-red despite it being a rainy day outside.

Five minutes later, another bell sounds, this one releasing us to first period. I want to look at Luke, maybe say something more, but I don't—I simply gather my things and rush from the room. All part of not knowing how to talk to boys—it's one thing when you're casual friends, but another when you've just said something that might make it seem like more.

He stays on my mind all day. I can't believe he's leaving in two short weeks—right after Valentine's Day.

4

FEBRUARY 9

Taylor

Maybe for most high school seniors, sitting at a table outside the cafeteria during lunch period to sell valentine wishes for the *Tribune* would be easy. For me, it's an act of courage I repeat several times a year: In fall, the paper sells "boo-grams," at the holidays it's "Christmas wishes," and for the February edition, we sell "heart wishes," messages that appear inside heart graphics in the paper.

While kids are giving me their dollar bills and writing out friendly or romantic Valentine's Day wishes, I'm sitting there *acting* normal but *really* wondering if I'm wearing the right jeans, if my shoes are cool enough, and if my curls are tame or comically out of control. Deep down I know none of it matters, but after years of ridicule, of people *acting* like it matters, well...it ends up mattering.

The only fun part is that it's become a wonderful use for my valentine box. The wishes are dropped inside so that anonymous ones really remain anonymous.

Last year, I clumsily spilled water in the box while working on the wishes at home and part of the bottom warped. Fortunately, though, it only showed on the inside, and over the past few days, I've given the whole box a makeover. I painted it red, and then last night Mom helped me decoupage the whole interior and lid using old school valentines I'd saved.

Now I wonder if she noticed they were all from the few girls who've ever been nice to me—and Luke Montgomery. "*Woof* you be my valentine?" Mom read out loud with a smile as she brushed the Mod Podge over it. "That's cute."

"Yeah," I said. "Cute." But what I really meant was *tragic*. As in sad. As in I've saved all the childish little valentines he gave me from fourth to eighth grade, as if they meant something. As in I've never had a boyfriend and the one I long for would never look at me like that, and besides, in a few days he's moving away forever.

"Hey, bestie," says Caroline in greeting, her eyes widening on me as she exits the lunchroom. Then she digs in her purse for a dollar. "One heart wish please." She looks very pleased with herself as she's writing it out, and I already know it's to me and will say something like: *To my very bestest friend.* She's a little clingy, but I love her for it. She's the only person who's ever clung to me in my life.

As she pushes it through the slot, it gets a little hung up, not dropping down. I make a face and tell her, "It's freshly decoupaged, so maybe it hasn't completely dried." Then I unlatch the lid and flip it over to look, touching a few spots with one fingertip. "But seems okay." *Whew*. Crisis averted. I've got enough problems without having to deal with an angry high schooler whose wish got mucked up and didn't appear in the paper.

"Okay, well, have fun!" Caroline says merrily and heads off down the hallway.

As if. "See you in biology," I answer instead.

Jasmine mostly quit bothering me after the eighth grade box-stealing incident but is still the queen bee of Sweetwater High. She's been chasing Luke for a couple of years—and could teach a course in how to talk to boys—but I've always noticed he doesn't date much, concentrating mostly on sports and horses. So Jasmine flirts with Luke but dates *other* guys.

Me, I'm always happy when she has a boyfriend, because it gives her something to focus on when life as cheerleader and prom queen isn't enough. For her, boredom equals bullying.

I heard yesterday that she broke up with Shawn Morell, and it must be true because as hallway traffic picks up, giving me a steady stream of customers, I spot her and a small swarm of worker bee girls gathered slightly down the hall, giggling and whispering with repeated looks in my direction. Great.

It could be anything. My previously-worried-about jeans, shoes, or hair. The top I'm wearing today. The fact that I'm still using the heart-shaped box she's always found so strangely hilarious. It's not my glasses because I talked my mom into contacts last year. (Though Jasmine found a way to make fun of that, too, on the first day of school. "Aw, red's trying to be like the rest of us. Isn't that just so cute?")

I ignore the stares and whispers, at least on the outside. On the inside, they grate. On the inside, they turn me back into that fourth grader with ink all over my shirt being laughed at by the other kids.

"It's a dollar," I reply when an underclassman asks.

"*It's a dollar*," I hear Jasmine mimic me. Like there's something ridicule-worthy about my answer.

When the traffic disperses a minute later, but the bees are still at it, I feel a little like I did that day in eighth grade. Like maybe she's gonna push me to a point of responding. Like *this,* added to Luke's impending departure and the center-of-attention vibe I suffer from sitting at this table, is just one thing too many.

That's when my eyes fall randomly on a warped spot on one of the wooden lunchroom doors directly across the hall from me. It's shaped like a heart on its side. It's probably been there longer than I've been a student here, but I've never noticed it until this moment.

I still see them, all the time. Usually when I need them, when I'm down or afraid or seeking answers. They always keep me going, and I've continued to believe they're from my dad, there to help me through life. And whereas the one I saw on the day Jasmine took my box inspired me to be brave and go after her, this one is giving me the opposite impression. It's telling me not to stoop to her level, that she's not worth it.

"If it's not Taylor Mulvaney, keeper of the heart wishes."

I look up to see Luke. He's stayed pretty glum since

finding out he has to move, an emotion reflected in his eyes right now, but he's trying to be cheerful. I smile up at him, a natural response, but it's not lost on me that Jasmine and her friends are watching. "Keeper of the heart wishes. I like that. I'll have to remember that for my future resume."

When he smiles back, it turns my skin hot. But then my heart sinks. Because he's almost out of my life. I feel the need to commiserate some more. "I still can't believe you're leaving."

He gives his head a discouraged shake. "Me neither. Sucks."

"This is your last week?"

He blows out a sad sigh. "Yep. The ballgame Friday night and the sweetheart dance on Saturday will be my last official acts as a student of Sweetwater High." Then he tilts his head. "You coming?"

He's never asked me that before—about anything. "Yeah, I'll be at the game." I go to *every* game, Caroline in tow, to watch him play.

"I meant the dance."

Oh. "Um, probably not." *Definitely* not. "Not really my thing." It's couples or big groups of friends, and I'm not part of either.

"*Could be* your thing. You should come."

I just look at him, eyes slightly narrowed. Does he truly not get it? Is he so accustomed to life as Luke Montgomery, popular guy, that he doesn't understand how, for me, a high school dance would equal walking in alone, standing alone, drinking punch alone, and then leaving alone? With maybe a few friendly words from a teacher chaperone who feels sorry for me? Or maybe I could drag Caroline kicking and screaming, but then we'd just be *two* losers standing by ourselves in a corner. "Like I said, not my thing. I don't really have anyone to go with. And I wouldn't have anything to wear."

"It's not formal or anything," he counters without missing a beat. "Just in the gym. And I'm sure you could find *someone* to hang out with." He's flashing me this cute—dare I even think almost flirtatious?—smile that suggests it really matters to him, that he *wants* me there. Is he saying *he'd* hang out with me?

But it's not enough. He'll cruise in with his buddies, and soon enough Jasmine and the other cheerleaders will be flocking around. And I'd walk in—again—by myself. (I'm really not sure I could talk Caroline into going.) So if he's thinking he'd come say hi, or even dance with me, it would still never work. No matter how tempting a dance in Luke's arms might be.

I'm not sure he realizes how different our lives are. He can saunter into an event and find dozens of people to chat with. Whereas my entire social circle consists of Caroline, the few girls in the baking club, and a handful of people on the newspaper staff who may or may not actually like me. Not good odds for a fun evening.

So I level with him—sort of. "Can't say I'd look forward to more of what's happening at this very moment that you aren't even aware of. Don't look now," I say, smiling yet frank, and breaking out the air quotes, "but your *friend* is doing that laughing-at-me-for-just-existing thing she enjoys. I get enough of that when I *have* to be on the premises."

He tosses a quick sideways glance in Jasmine's direction,

then turns a playful expression back my way. "I told you, she's not my friend. She's—"

We say it together. *"Part of my friend group."* And both laugh. It's been our ongoing joke all through high school. Even if it's not very funny.

I know he's between a social rock and a hard place—but it still stings to know he hangs out with her despite how awful she is, even if it's in a group. I'm not sure what I expect him to do; I'm not sure what *I'd* do in his position—it's pretty easy to follow the path of least resistance. Yet it's still difficult to watch.

It's then that he drops a glance to my valentine box, then raises his eyes to the poster board sign taped to the wall behind me. "So these wishes are a dollar, huh?"

I nod.

Digging in his pocket, he hands me a dollar bill and starts to write one out.

Of course, I suffer the wild urge to know what it says. I'm praying it's not for Jasmine. But I'm too smart to think it's for me. Guess I'll find out when I go through them after school.

"Two wishes please, Taylor," says a freshman girl in our baking club named Fiona, stepping up to hold out two bucks. "How long can they be? And when will this issue of the paper come out?"

I answer her questions, vaguely aware of Luke doing an awfully lot of writing the whole time. I only get to glance back his way when he's stuffing the paper slip through the slot.

"I better get going. Lunch break's over," he tells me with another small grin, pointing vaguely up the hall.

Fiona wrote hers out quick and now shoves them in as well—and they get stuck a little, too, like Caroline's. So instead of leaving, Luke reaches down to push the protruding slips of paper the rest of the way in—at the exact same time I do, and our fingers touch. It's only a few seconds, during which I try to act normal, but it ricochets through my body like a tingly pinball, the best feeling I've ever had.

Fiona has already walked away, and I'm suddenly overcome by...everything. Loss. Desire. Intense affection. And fear. But I move past the last one to say, "I'm gonna miss you, Luke."

"I'm gonna miss you, too, Taylor."

And then he's gone. Up the hall.

Word of the day: *Sadness.* It's not a *funny* word—but like when Luke was angry, just what's overwhelming me right now.

And even as my chest aches with the anticipated loss, I become aware of Jasmine Dupree in my peripheral vision, rolling her eyes at her friends as if to say: *She can't seriously think he likes her.*

Do I?

Or maybe the bigger question is: Does it even matter?

In a few days, I'll never see Luke Montgomery again.

That night, after a call from Mom on her break and some leftover meatloaf from the diner, heated in the microwave, I sit down at our little kitchen table, ready to get to work on the heart wishes. Unlatching and sliding the lid carefully off the box, I set it aside, then dump the wish slips into a big pile on the table. I return the box's lid and carry it to my room, situating it on a shelf like a knickknack and feeling a little down because I'm not sure what else I'll ever use it for. I've always liked that it had a purpose, even if only a once-a-year purpose, because my dad was a man who took pleasure in knowing the things he built were utilized in some way. But maybe the valentine box will only be a decoration now.

On my way back to the table, I grab a notebook and pen, ready to transcribe the wishes. Tomorrow I'll collect the ones sold by the rest of the staff and stay after school, typing them up before the following day's deadline.

But after I write out the first few, I realize I'm hoping every slip I pick up is Luke's, because I want to know who his wish is for. It's stayed in the back of my mind all afternoon, and part of me can't believe I resisted looking until now.

So I start rifling through them. Seems like I'm always searching the communications dropped in that box for something from Luke Montgomery.

Then I find it:

From: Luke Montgomery
My wish: Hope all my friends and classmates have an awesome Valentine's Day. I love this school and I'm going to miss you all!

Well, it *was* a lot to write, which explains why he took so long. And the wish makes perfect sense. Not sure what else I was expecting.

5

FEBRUARY 14

Luke

7:15 p.m.

I'm early to the sweetheart dance. Well, earlier than normal anyway. I know how these things go down. Doors open at seven, but it's dead until seven-thirty or eight. My usual crew rolls in fashionably late—eight or after. That's why I wrote 7:15 on that extra slip of paper I dropped in Taylor's heart-shaped box.

Am I a coward to have waited this long, until literally the night before I'm leaving Sweetwater, probably forever? Is that what it took for me to decide it doesn't matter what my friends think? And what the hell is my grand plan here anyway? Since I am, in fact, moving tomorrow.

The fact that I'm starting at a new school in less than forty-eight hours is enough to make my stomach pinch up a little, but I need to focus on now, and the fact that I'm watching the wide row of doors leading into the gym lobby, waiting for her to walk through one of them. I'm holding a dozen red roses, trying to do this right.

I didn't plan to ask her—but as I stood there talking to her outside the cafeteria, it hit me how much I like her, and how much more fun I'd have with her than any of my friends—male or female. So I followed the impulse to write out one of those wish slips to her, from me, asking her to be my date.

Which brings me back to that grand plan I don't have. What if we have an amazing time? What if holding her while we dance feels as good as I think it will? What if I kiss her and that's good, too? And then I have to leave.

Maybe we could keep in touch? I could always drive back to see her on weekends or during the summer.

But hold up there, Mario Andretti—you're getting ahead of yourself. Let's just see how the date goes.

I don't usually get nervous before dates, but I'm a little on edge. I suggested meeting early to take the pressure off, so she wouldn't feel uncomfortable walking in with a crowd, so we could connect without anyone coming up to talk. I hope she gets here soon.

7:30 p.m.

I stand to one side of the lobby, by the trophy cases, watching the doors even closer now, anticipation mounting inside me each time one opens. I'm waiting for that moment: when the person who's late finally arrives, and you feel so good, because you knew they were coming, but maybe there was one tiny part of you beginning to wonder.

Only Taylor doesn't seem like someone who runs late. In fact, I'd have bet on her to be the type who shows up early.

Then again, maybe she struggled over what to wear—I know she's not comfortable with this kind of event. I'm in dress khakis and a navy jacket over a button-down shirt—same thing I wore to my cousin's wedding last fall. But I don't care if she shows up in tattered blue jeans—I just want her to get here.

7:45 p.m.

Crowds are picking up now, more kids arriving. I hang in the shadows when I see TJ come in. I don't want to have to explain who the flowers are for. Jasmine has been hinting all week for me to ask her to the dance—I don't need him assuming I'm suddenly into her.

I figured when Taylor got here, we'd just walk in arm and arm, get some punch or whatever, and then I'd ask her to dance. And when my friends started coming up, I'd act like it was totally normal that I'm with her. I'd say something like, "Taylor's my date tonight," or "I asked Taylor to the dance." They're good guys—they'd be fine with it, just surprised.

But every time a door opens and someone else walks through, I have to begin facing something that never even crossed my mind: She's not coming.

She didn't say anything about it when I saw her the last few days, but she still gave me her usual shy smile. It made me think she just didn't want to talk about it; that same as I asked her in a sort of quiet, secret way, she wanted to answer by just showing up. And she wasn't even in homeroom yesterday—late because a school bus broke down. I didn't think it mattered; I figured I'd see her tonight.

But damn. Maybe she's really standing me up.

Is it standing me up if she never actually agreed to the date in the first place?

But if she wasn't gonna come, she could have at least told me—tucked a note in my backpack, *something*.

My face starts getting hot. Did I really misread all our conversations? Was I the only one who thought we were flirting lately? Is she really turning me down by ignoring my invitation altogether?

God, I'm an idiot.

I guess my dad's right—I'm pretty full of myself. Maybe I thought every girl liked me. That's kind of been my experience so far. But now I feel like a loser. To have assumed.

I actually imagined the moment when she found my note in the wishes. I thought she'd be excited, that maybe she'd nibble her lower lip the way I've seen her do when something goes well for her—like she isn't quite sure she believes it at first, but then she does, and her green eyes get bright and wide and kind of beautiful. I imagined her going through her closet, finding just the right thing to wear.

But I guess she only sees me as a friend. And maybe she was actually...*horrified* to find the note.

The paper with the heart wishes came out yesterday, so I know she went through them all, but I don't know when. Maybe if I'd seen her in homeroom yesterday, she would have acted weird because of it. Or maybe she just decided to ignore the whole thing. After all, I'm leaving, so it's not like she ever has to see me again. Maybe that seemed like the easiest answer: *no* answer. Just leave me standing here like a fool.

The thought makes me shrink back into the shadows a little deeper as I look around, wondering if anyone sees the dumb guy holding roses for a girl who isn't gonna show.

No matter how I slice it, though, it's hard to believe she'd do that to me—just leave me waiting, every minute like an eternity. I thought she was a nicer person than that.

Or...is this how to you pay someone back for not defending you enough, for letting the person who's mean to you just skate by? Maybe she thinks it serves me right.

And maybe it does.

8:00 p.m.

Okay, I know she's not coming, so why am I still holding this bouquet and staring at the stupid doors? It's been—I check a clock on the wall—forty-five minutes. Maybe I just keep hoping I'm wrong.

All right, one more time. I'm gonna watch one more door open and one more person walk through. And if it's not her, I'm outta here.

When I see a door begin to move, I wish with everything

in me. *Please, please, please.* Talk about a heart wish—this gives the term a whole new meaning.

Then a slender blonde in a barely-there dress that looks more like lingerie walks in: Jasmine. And even though no one else has seemed to notice me standing here in the lobby this whole time, her eyes land on me instantly.

She sashays up in sky-high heels that make her as tall as me, her lipstick the same cotton-candy pink as the heart design on her slinky dress. "Are those for me?"

She's talking about the flowers, obviously, but her gaze brims with invitation.

Hell. She's gorgeous, she's been chasing me around for years, and—unlike the girl I actually bought the roses for—she wants to go to this dance with me.

"Sure," I murmur, handing her the armful of flowers.

She takes them, then leans in, pressing her barely-concealed breasts against my arm to say, "And here I almost thought you were gonna leave town without us ever getting together. I'm glad you came to your senses."

Taylor

The Sweetheart Diner has been my home away from home ever since my dad died five years ago—mainly because that's where my mom spends most of her time, waiting tables. Dad had enough life insurance to bury him, and we get social security, but it's not enough.

It's less than a quarter-mile from our house—which was convenient before I had my driver's license, and still is some-times in the summer if I just feel like walking.

The truth is, I don't know how the place stays in business with less and less action on Main Street. But I appreciate getting paid to bake cakes and pies on the weekends. I love getting lost in the mixing and decorating—it takes me away from my troubles. And it's kind of fun working in a bigger kitchen than the ones at home or school.

The only thing "sweetheartish" about the place is a couple of hearts on the laminated menu, and *The Sweetheart Diner* painted in script on the wall in red, matching the red vinyl booths and stools. I know the business name was drawn from the town name, but I've always thought Walt could do more with the theme.

Not that it's any of my business. My business is baking desserts and spending the rest of my time here in the back booth reading or doing homework. Which is what I'm attempting when Mom's waitress friend, Geneva, approaches me, wiping her hands on her apron.

Geneva is short, stout, sturdy, and hardworking, but what I love most about her is that she dyes her short hair red—an even redder shade than mine—by choice! I'm not sure it's the best color for her, but she does what she wants and I admire that. I can only hope I'm as self-possessed as Geneva by the time I'm in my fifties. "What has you so deep in thought?" she asks.

"World War I," I reply, gesturing to the open history book before me.

But it's a lie.

Which she can apparently tell, because she says, "I thought maybe it was that boy."

All she and Mom know is that there's a boy at school I

like, but that he's way out of my league and nothing will ever come of it. No way could I say who because everyone knows Luke Montgomery by virtue of his father being the town doctor. In fact, the Montgomerys have been a big topic of discussion lately because, until someone buys Dr. M.'s practice, we'll all have to drive a lot farther when we're sick.

"No," I lie again, trying to sound light and casual about it.

I'm not sure it works, but she lets it go and starts wiping down tables. Mom stands behind the counter consolidating ketchup bottles and refilling napkin dispensers.

A glance at the clock on the wall tells me it's ten, with an hour until closing. No one comes in this late, ever, and I've also always thought Walt could save a little money by shutting down earlier.

I've spent way too much time the last few days thinking about Luke and the dance he's at right now. After our conversation outside the lunchroom, I wondered if I should change my mind and go. I even found myself fantasizing about it.

By digging through my mother's closet, I discover some fabulous-not-tacky vintage 1980s dress, red taffeta, strapless, that complements my coloring perfectly. My mom puts my hair in some kind of up-do, with little tendrils curling down around my face, and I look prettier than ever in my life.

Brave but humble, I walk through the gym doors. Every eye turns to look at the new arrival, stunned to see that it's me and I'm suddenly a knockout. My gaze locks with Luke's and he starts toward me. Appearing wowed by my stunning transformation, he tells me I look beautiful.

Then I hear the first notes of "Lady in Red." (This part is even more far-fetched than the rest because it's a song from the

8os that most people my age have never heard, but it's my fantasy, and that's how it happens.) And Luke holds out his hand to ask, "May I have this dance?"

I answer by placing my hand in his and we step onto the dance floor. He pulls me close, our bodies pressing together from chest to thigh. He looks into my eyes, and then there's kissing. I've never been kissed, but that makes it even more perfect—and turns out I'm a natural at it.

When the song ends, he tells me his father changed his mind and they're not leaving after all, and he asks me to be his girlfriend. I say yes and the credits roll.

Because this is basically just a teen movie, full of unlikelihoods that never really happen in real life. But it's nice to think about anyway.

Or *kind of* nice. Since maybe it just makes the reality a little harder. The reality that he likes me enough to say I should come to the dance, but not enough to ditch his buddies for me or anything. The reality that he's just a decent guy being nice to the girl without many friends. The reality that I'll never see him again because my bus was late on Friday, so I didn't even get to say goodbye. I went to the basketball game last night with Caroline as planned, watching from the bleachers as Luke scored twelve points off the bench—but it's not like he knew or cared that I was there.

Of course, it's occurred to me that maybe the bus breakdown was fated. It saved me from possibly doing or saying something embarrassing, or even just getting unduly emotional as I said goodbye. Maybe God or the universe was actually doing me a favor.

All of that is mostly what I'm thinking about as I sit trying to focus on my history assignment—my ill-fated crush on the most popular boy in school who's leaving town tomorrow.

When the bell on the diner's door jangles, Mom, Geneva, and I all look up, surprised. Like I said, no one ever comes in this late.

So it's almost beyond my ability to comprehend when TJ, Courtney, Billy, and the whole jock crowd come in—including Luke and Jasmine. Jasmine is leaning on Luke, her arm looped through his, even as they walk through the door. My heart drops to my stomach.

As a group of seven, all dressed to the nines, squeeze into a booth a few away from mine, with one of the guys pulling over a chair from a four-top table, I wish I was anywhere else. For so, so many reasons, but mainly because it suddenly feels like it's all been a lie. *She's just in my friend group.* How many times has he said that to me? But right now she's hanging all over him, whispering something to him with a giggle, and he clearly likes it. Lucky me that they sat on the side facing my table.

It's as my mother takes their drink orders, and I'm wondering if I could somehow slink unseen out the back door, that Luke notices me. And as our eyes meet, I wait for it: that cute, playful shrug of "looks like I got stuck with her," or the scrunch of his nose to imply he'd rather be sitting with me, or even just a little wave. Even when he's with his friends, he always smiles or says hi when we pass in the hall.

So when he instead flashes me a dirty look, it's like a punch in the gut. His eyes narrow and his features twist into a scowl of disgust—an expression I've never seen on his face before—and it's aimed directly at *me*. The rest of them ignore me as though we haven't all gone to school together for eight years, and right now, maybe I wish he were ignoring me, too—because this is much worse.

My jaw drops and I simply gape at him, astonished and confused. I blink a few times, then mouth the words: *What's wrong?*

In response, he simply rolls his eyes like I've done something abominable.

Then he turns and kisses Jasmine Dupree! Not a little kiss, either. The kind...well, the kind I fantasized about sharing with him on the dance floor. Suddenly my fantasy seems more impossible than ever and Jasmine's words from years ago echo in my head: *Can't you just see her, blushing and fantasizing, thinking they really like her? I wonder who she has the biggest crush on.*

Their friends hoot and holler at the passionate kiss that's making me sick to my stomach. When it ends, Jasmine appears victorious, and I want the black and white checkerboard floor of the Sweetheart Diner to open up and swallow me whole.

Someone jokes, "I guess we know who's driving Jas home tonight," and everyone laughs. Except me. Thank God they're ignoring me because my face is surely fifty shades of red by now.

Quietly closing my book and gathering my things, I scoot swiftly from the booth and make a beeline for the kitchen. I pass my mom at the soda machine and can tell she knows something's wrong. She stops running drinks and follows me. Before I know it, I'm standing there surrounded by Mom,

Geneva, and Walt, probably looking like the end of the world has come.

"Honey, what is it? What's wrong?" Mom asks. All three look worried.

I can only shake my head. If I try to speak, I'll cry. I feel so stupid. To be like this over a boy who only ever showed me a little kindness, nothing more. But why is he suddenly being horrible to me? And to see him kissing my arch enemy—it's a lot.

Tossing a surreptitious glance out the long, narrow pass-through window, Geneva then turns back to the rest of us and says quietly, "I think I know who the boy is now."

My mother's eyes go wide as she whispers, "Dr. Montgomery's son?"

I'm mortified, even in front of the people who care about me. Because Luke is…Luke. And I'm me. It's embarrassing for them to know I have feelings for a guy who would never look twice at me in that way.

That's when Walt, bald and stocky and someone who's always been kind but not overly personal with me, changes that by lifting my downcast chin with one bent finger. "Now you listen to me, young lady," he says, voice low enough for only the four of us to hear. "Any boy who doesn't see what a gem you are isn't worth your time, and that's the God's honest truth. Don't you give him, or any of those kids, another thought."

It's incredibly sweet—and so of course I burst into tears.

Walt says, "Aw, honey—come here," and pulls me into a hug.

My mother is rubbing my shoulder as Geneva tells her,

"I'll get the drinks and take the orders." But then she leans closer to say, "Walt's right, hon. You hang in there, and everything'll be okay."

After that, Walt lets Mom off early, and we sneak out the back through the kitchen to where Mom parks. We go home and eat ice cream straight from the tub and I tell her my entire past with Luke Montgomery. She replies with things like she knows it hurts but I won't feel that way forever and that after high school everything changes and people see you differently. Then she uses one hand to push back my hair, closing with, "I know none of that helps much right now, though."

A little while later I cry myself to sleep, still shattered, and at the same time almost glad I'll never see him again.

Word of the day: *Heartbreak.*

Senior Year of College

FEBRUARY 14

Taylor

I don't have classes today, and Mom has recently left her job at the diner after eight years, so she's home, too. We're going through closets and cabinets, cleaning things out.

She's getting remarried in two weeks and moving an hour away, near Louisville, but the little house where I've grown up will be mine for as long as I want it to be. Through all of Mom's late hours at the diner, she managed to pay off the mortgage early, just before the holidays, so she could make it a Christmas gift to me. She never told me until then, or I wouldn't have let her do it. Nonetheless, it's reassuring to know I have a free place to live and the money from the house if I ever sell it. It's a *big* gift. I think she feels guilty about leaving, and guilty about Dad's death and other things in my life she had no control over.

I still live at home, going to community college three days a week while waiting tables and baking at the diner on other days. I graduate in May and plan to stay here until I find a good job and figure out adult life.

"You can always come live with David and me," Mom tells me again as she hefts a box down from the living room closet shelf. "It's a big house, there are plenty of bedrooms, and his kids only come every other weekend."

"I'll bear it in mind," I say, same as always. It's a generous offer, and David's a great guy. He owns a gorgeous five-bedroom home in the kind of upscale neighborhood I could only ever dream of living in. But I want Mom to get the fresh start she deserves, so I need to find my way on my own. I'm about to earn a bachelor's degree in business, which should help. Too bad the only thing I really love to do is bake. I haven't seen too many high-paying positions on the internet for bakers.

Mom sets the cardboard box in an old recliner and opens it up to say, "Oh, look! The valentine box your dad made for you."

When she pulls it out, I gasp. So many memories are tied up in that box, more than I ever imagined on the day he gave it to me on the way to school. I take it from her, the very sight making me miss Dad. "I forgot how beautiful this is. I should at least have it out on a table or something." It was for a while, but as my little room became more cramped with books, a computer, and all the stuff that accumulates throughout life, I packed it away with some other tchotchkes when we decided to paint the room, and I never got any of them back out.

Feeling the urge to peek inside—because the decoupaged kids' valentines make the interior as interesting as the exterior —I carefully unlatch the wooden lid and lift it off. But before I can even look, I'm stopped by an unexpected knock on the door.

Mom opens it to find Walt on our front stoop. In all the years we've known Walt, he's never come to our house. "Walt. Hi." As she steps back to let him in, I feel our collective concern. We're both hoping nothing is wrong, that no one has died or the diner hasn't gone into foreclosure or something.

After niceties, he removes a knitted winter hat from his bald head and holds it in front of him in both hands, fumbling with it uncomfortably. "I'll get to the point of why I'm here," he says. "I thought I owed it to both of you to tell you in person that I'm closing up shop, retiring. Business is down more than ever and Sweetwater just can't support a diner anymore. With you leaving after all these years, Lisa, it just feels like time. I talked to my wife and we're gonna get a little cabin out in the country, and maybe a camper—do a little traveling."

The truth is, Walt is probably pushing seventy, so this makes all the sense in the world, for many reasons, but I'm certain I look just as shocked as Mom.

"I know this leaves you in the lurch, Taylor," he goes on, "and I'm very sorry. That's my one regret, that you and Geneva and the rest of the staff will be out of work. Planning on the end of May, by the way. I hope that gives you time to make some other plans, and I know that's when you're graduating." He's still fiddling with his hat so much that I'm afraid he'll wear a hole in it.

"Anyway, I'm calling Dupree Realty tomorrow, and it'll be priced to sell if you know anyone who'd want an old diner in an old town no one comes to anymore." He ends on an ironic, unsmiling sort of laugh.

And that's when a probably crazy question enters my mind. But I'm literally holding a heart in my hand, so maybe that makes it less crazy. Because all these years later, I still see them everywhere—in clouds and tree bark and rocks and even oil stains in the street.

Though maybe this doesn't count as a sign—even if Dad *made* the heart, it's a heart that's *supposed* to be a heart; it's not something I'm seeing where others might not. It's just a coincidence.

Even so, as I glance down at it between my hands, I hear myself ask, "How much?"

"How much what?" Walt replies.

I tilt my head, smiling inwardly. Walt simply never *was* much of a businessman—he just liked running a diner. "How much would you sell it for?"

Now it's Walt tipping his head to one side. "You know someone?"

I scrunch up my nose, shake my head. I'm a little embarrassed. "No, I've just...always wished I could open a little bake shop somewhere."

Walt looks sad as he informs me, "Not sure Sweetwater is the place for it, kiddo. I love ya and that's why I'm being honest, lookin' out for ya. Afraid it'd be a losing proposition, no matter how delicious all your sweet treats are."

I just let out a sigh. "Yeah, I know. A girl can dream, though, right?"

He nods. "Listen now—don't let an old man crush your ambitions. Just dream about that shop someplace else." He ends on a wink.

After more apologies and some hugs, Walt leaves. And Mom and I plop down on the couch, digesting this information. My stomach churns. "The one thing I thought I could depend on was my job at the diner."

Mom reaches over and grabs my hand, giving it a squeeze. "Don't worry—we'll figure it out. You know David has offered to get you an admin position at his company. He told me just last night the offer still holds."

He's an executive at a large corporation that makes apparel for restaurants—like the embroidered polo shirts and aprons we wear at the diner. It seems full circle—for Mom anyway. And I guess it could be for me, too. An easy answer.

Only I was hoping for something that felt more...me. Something I'd feel excited about.

But I suppose *everyone* hopes for that—and probably not a lot of people get it.

"I'll think about it," I tell her.

Up to now, that's just been lip service, but without my job at the diner, maybe I need to consider it more seriously. Our little river town has become less and less populated, and the impending closure of the diner feels like one more nail in its coffin.

At some point, I lowered the valentine box to the coffee

table, the lid off but tilted against it to one side. Although my mind is in other places right now, I reach over and pick up both pieces, drawing the box into my lap. I study the childish valentines pasted on the bottom and inner sides, overlapping one another randomly. I spot one from Caroline; another from Luke Montgomery. *Woof you be my valentine?*

I guess I haven't looked in this box since high school, but something I always thought would be a sweet memory has now become a bitter one. I never found out why he was so mean after the sweetheart dance. I never saw him again after that weird, ugly incident in the diner. But the look on his face that night haunts me even now.

Then I flip over the lid to study the old valentines decoupaged there, as well. Only...what am I seeing? A small slip of white paper appears stuck there, near the slot, protruding from beneath the corner of a valentine not quite glued all the way to the wood. I reach for it, but it's definitely attached.

"What's that?" Mom asks.

"I'm not sure. Maybe one of those heart wishes I used to sell for the paper. I remember some getting sort of stuck the last time I used the box."

"Hadn't we just glued all the old valentines inside?"

I think back, trying to remember. "Yeah—I don't think it had dried properly. I guess someone never got their wish delivered." Tugging gently at the folded slip as I speak, I finally free it, though one edge rips, leaving a small bit behind.

I open the piece of paper.

From: Luke to Taylor
My wish: Is that you'll be my date to the sweetheart
dance even though it's not your thing. Meet me by
the trophy case at 7:15. We'll have fun, I promise.

"Oh my God," I mutter. I just stare at it. "This can't be real. Can it?"

Mom is looking over my shoulder as I blink, twice, and read it again to make sure it says what I think it says.

"I think it's real," Mom replies. Then adds another, "Oh my God."

I look at her, mouth gaping. "I can't believe it. He asked me to the dance. He asked me to the dance and I didn't go."

Mom blows out a sigh, but lifts both hands in a wait-a-minute gesture. "To be fair, though, he didn't exactly go about it in the most direct way. I mean, did it never occur to him that you might not see it? That it could get lost or mixed up with all the other slips of paper?"

"Apparently not," I answer, remembering that horrible look he gave me. Now I understand, though, why that kiss he planted on Jasmine seemed almost designed to spite me. "But this sure explains a lot."

"If you want to know what I think," Mom says, "it was dumb of him to leap to conclusions."

I can't disagree. Though what I'm still stuck on is, "I can't believe he really wanted to take me to that dance. I can't believe he thought I totally ignored it!"

"You could Google him," Mom suggests. The Montgomery family indeed all left town the next day and we haven't heard anything about them since. Their farm never sold, and some out-of-town company takes care of the lawn and the house, and from what I've heard, no one in Sweetwater has had any contact with them other than an occasional sighting of Mrs. Montgomery at the property. Luke's old friends are probably still in touch with him, but they're all away in school and their parents just aren't people I chitchat with.

As for why I've never Googled him before, I was leaving the past in the past. But the past just became mired with a missed invitation. So I set the valentine box aside and pick up my cell phone as Mom peers over my shoulder.

The upshot is that a number of guys named Luke Montgomery come up when I search, but none of them are him. Dr. Montgomery remains at a practice in Cincinnati, and when I search on Luke's brothers, they, too, appear—one's become an attorney and the other also seems to be pursuing a law degree, at Emory in Atlanta. But no Luke.

I keep looking, though—and part of me hates that I'm doing it, taking Googling to the deep-dive level, but Mom says nothing to stop me. I guess, given what I've just discovered, she understands why I'd want to find him.

Then I take a slightly more extreme step—I start Googling his old friends. I find TJ as a senior at UK, as I would have *expected* Luke to be right now. Same for the other guys I look for, and a few come up on social media, but none of their posts mention Luke.

And that's when I break down and type into the search bar: *Jasmine Dupree.*

Behind me, my mother makes a hissing noise—her way of

asking without asking: *Are you sure you really want to go there?*

I'm not sure at all, but I do it. And I end up on Jasmine's social media. And I see the worst thing I could possibly imagine: a picture of a still-flawless Jasmine with a still-handsome Luke. As always, he could use a haircut, but these days he looks more rugged than athletic, sporting a thin, light brown beard. And he's wearing a cowboy hat.

The caption: *Visiting my hot boyfriend in Utah. Have to leave tomorrow—wah! But I'll be back on spring break! The view out here is stunning, and I don't mean just the landscape. Be jealous, ladies, because he's all mine.*

I barely know what to make of it. A cowboy hat? Utah? A beard? All reminders that I never really knew him very well.

And as for this whole being-Jasmine's-boyfriend business, it wrenches my stomach—partly because maybe it wouldn't be like that if I'd found his invitation and gone to the stupid dance.

But, okay, maybe it also would. Because whatever's happened between then and now, last I knew, they were going off to the same college in the same "friend group," so maybe it was just meant to be.

"Well, that's that," I mutter. I shut down the app, set down my phone, and wipe my palms one over the other a few times, washing my hands of the whole affair.

My mom says nothing for a moment, but as my gaze drops to the valentine box once more, she offers up, "Well, if you were thinking he'd ever come back, this makes it seem less likely. I'm not saying you were—I have no idea. But if that weighs into it at all, we can talk to David about possibilities for you after graduation."

I take a deep breath, blow it back out. Was I? Thinking he might come back someday? I honestly have no idea. But if I was, she's right—this kind of seals it. Utah might as well be the moon.

And Walt's leaving. And Mom's leaving.

Maybe I should leave, too.

After all, why would I want to stick around this dying old river town?

It's odd, though—something happened that I never expected. Despite everything I've hated about living in Sweetwater through the years, somewhere along the way, it became home.

10 Years Later

JANUARY 5

Taylor

I stand behind the big glass display case at the Sweetheart Bake Shop on a typical winter weekday morning. By the time of my college graduation, Walt had gotten no nibbles on the diner, so he offered it to me at a rock-bottom price I couldn't resist.

Even though I didn't have any money.

David helped me out with an interest-free loan which he kindly called a graduation present—he's a truly awesome guy who's been making my mom very happy for ten years now.

Crazy how time passes—it feels like yesterday that I pulled my little business together and hung out a shingle for the Sweetheart Bake Shop, where we have a very simple business model: we make only heart-shaped baked goods. Cakes, pies, cookies, brownies, cupcakes – all shaped like hearts. With pink pastel hearts painted on the walls, and pink vinyl booths and chairs, I have embraced and combined the "sweet" in Sweetwater, the Sweetheart Diner legacy, and the hearts that continue to tie me to my father—and I may not be getting rich, but it brings me joy every day.

I look up when the door opens and TJ Browerton walks in. "Morning, Taylor. Can I get three dozen cookies? Whatever you have is fine. Staff meeting today after school." TJ, once-upon-a-time jock in my class, is now the Sweetwater High football coach and a science teacher. He's still attractive, but in a more low-key way, now wearing glasses and sporting a tie beneath a half-zip sweater. He's always been a decent guy, and as adults, we're friendly acquaintances.

"Sure, TJ," I say, grabbing up a pink bakery box and a pair of tongs. I make small talk with him about the weather— it snowed a little over the weekend, but now it's just plain cold—as I fill the box with a mix of chocolate chip, peanut butter, and sugar cookies. On the other side of the interior window behind me, Geneva is busy baking, and my other full-time employee, nineteen-year-old Kyra, boxes up internet orders.

That's our secret sauce, how we stay in business—online orders. Using moisture-seal packaging, we mail our heart cookies and cupcakes all over the country. It's still a challenge to stay solvent, but the website customers help. And we've also become a bit of a regional destination when someone wants that perfect, pretty heart-shaped dessert for a special occasion.

As for the rest of Sweetwater's Main Street, it's more

empty than ever. My longtime best friend opened Sweet Caroline's Deli across the street five years ago (against everyone's advice, including mine), and she's struggling, too. Big box stores caused the initial decline decades back, but having a new one built even closer just two years ago has made the situation worse. Other than Caroline and me, all that's left on Main is a barber shop and an old timey drugstore barely hanging on by a thread. Every other storefront sits sadly empty.

The valentine box, currently painted pink, rests on the counter. As TJ steps over to the register to pay, he drops a business card in for a weekly chance to win a cake or pie. Once again, the box has found a use and I love that it's on display for every customer to see.

"Oh, I almost forgot," he says. "My mom needs a T-shirt —says her old one finally wore out. Told her I'd pick it up. Large."

"Great," I say, grabbing a tee from a shelf behind the counter and packaging it separately in a small pink shopping bag. Back when I first opened, people kept coming in thinking it was still a diner, so as kind of a joke, but also for real, I got pink T-shirts made that say, *Sweetheart Bake Shop (Not a Diner!)* for the staff, and they became a hit with some of the locals as well. We still wear them even now, mainly because every now and then, someone still comes in trying to order a burger and fries.

"How's Mags today?" TJ asks after I tell him the total. He drops a glance to my elderly pup, a curly white miniature poodle named Maggie, where she lies curled up in her pink doggie bed near the front window, fast asleep. Mags is mostly blind and doesn't have many teeth. She showed up outside the shop one day a few years ago, and what was I gonna do, leave her to fend for herself? Knowing that life in this town can be cruel, I took her in and she's become the bake shop mascot.

"Hanging in there," I reply, casting her an affectionate glance. "I'm surprised she didn't wake up when you came in." She might not be able to see, but she knows my regular customers by scent even amidst all the sweet smells of cakes and brownies.

He slants another look her way. "Bet this'll do it," he says, twisting the lid off the cookie jar labeled *Maggie's Hearts* near the register, then plucking out a heart-shaped doggie treat.

And indeed, the telltale sound perks Maggie awake, and a second later she's on her feet, lifting her front paws to the wall of her little gated area. Her tongue lolls from her mouth and her tail wags eagerly as she waits.

For purposes of cleanliness, we avoid petting her during business hours and leave that to the customers, so I'm pleased when TJ not only slips her the bacon-flavored treat, but also reaches down to scratch beneath her chin. I know she'd survive at home during the day, but I suspect she was abandoned more than once in her life, so I don't like to leave her alone for long stretches if I don't have to.

As TJ walks out, Caroline whisks in. Still a few dress sizes bigger than some consider the ideal, my beautiful friend came into her own after high school. She loves to dabble in makeup and piercings, is dating three different guys from out of town, and every New Year declares what her signature color of the year will be.

Shrugging free of her new purple coat (that's this year's color), she greets a tail-wagging Mags with a belly rub and baby-voiced, "There's my Maggie girl," then parks herself at the table nearest the door, her usual spot when she drops by before opening the deli for lunch.

That's when her normally cheerful expression—apparently only for Maggie today—transforms into an all-out scowl as she flips long, dark hair over her shoulder and addresses the shop at large. "Did you hear the news?"

I exchange glances with Geneva and Kyra through the window behind me. It would seem none of us have. "What news?"

"Well, rather than tell you, I can let you just see for yourself. Across the street, at eleven o'clock walking briskly toward ten."

I look—and can't believe my eyes.

Behind me, the other two crane to see, but the angle isn't right, so Geneva asks, "Who is it?"

I'm stunned by the words that leave my mouth. "Jasmine Dupree is walking down the street in a salmon-colored pantsuit."

"Oh dear," Geneva says.

As Kyra asks, "Who's Jasmine Dupree?"

Caroline answers, "Taylor's high school bully and nemesis. Mine, too, kind of, but she stole Taylor's man."

"Whoa," I say, holding up both hands, glad the attention-grabbing sight is now out of my vision. "He was, in no stretch of the imagination, my man." Then I look to Kyra. "Just a boy I had a crush on."

"And she looks ridiculous, if you ask me," Caroline adds, eyes back on Jasmine.

But I counter, "No, actually, she looks amazing. I could never pull off that outfit, but on her it was incredible."

"Well, it looks ridiculous *here*," Caroline clarifies.

Fair enough. I meet her halfway with, "It's a bit much for a dying Kentucky river town, I agree."

"And she also looked as miserable as ever, didn't you think?"

"She did always seem kind of miserable for a girl who had it all, didn't she?" I concur, scrunching my nose up slightly. "What on earth is she doing back in Sweetwater?"

Caroline presses her lips together in a flat, straight line, her eyes going I've-got-the-scoop wide. Then she holds up one finger. "Wait. First, a little backstory for Kyra. What we last knew was that Jasmine and Luke—that's the guy—were a couple in college, but he was in Utah and she was here. I'm not sure how that worked. But anyway, at some point—we don't know when—they broke up and she ended up in L.A. as some kind of assistant at a high-profile talent agency. She became a social media influencer because she was always at Hollywood parties, posting pictures of celebrities, and of herself looking fabulous. But then, *scandal*." The word comes out in a tone of salacious wonder.

"What happened?" Kyra asks, her hazel eyes as big as Caroline's now as she shoves back a tendril of long brown hair that's escaped her ponytail.

"According to my mother," Caroline says, "she got fired

from her job after fooling around with an older, married guy at her company. She lost a lot of her following, and she'd spent all her money on her lavish lifestyle, so she was bordering on broke and had no choice but to come home. At first it looked like she was just here for Christmas—but then she didn't leave and word starting getting around. Mom says she's doing admin work at her mother's office." Janet Dupree's real estate agency is down the street and around the corner in a well-kept colonial-style home and is probably the only business in Sweetwater that continues to thrive, because most of her listings come from other communities.

"That's quite a story," Geneva remarks, having joined the wide-eyed crew.

"All I can say," Caroline adds more quietly, "is that this town was a much nicer place without her."

And I can't argue the point. In fact, all the mean girls in her group eventually left for parts unknown, lifting away a certain veil of resentment that can persist over such things even in adulthood.

But surely Jasmine Dupree and I can co-exist peacefully —or at least avoid each other for however long she's here. Even if the sight of her out my plate-glass windows did send a little jolt of teenage PTSD skittering through my body.

That's when my phone buzzes with a text notification. Checking it, I say to the group, "It's Mom. She wants to know if I've seen yesterday's *Sweetwater Times*." Despite no longer living here, she still subscribes to keep up with town happenings. "And I haven't."

A glance around tells me no one is aware of whatever *this* news is, either—not even Caroline.

"She says to look on page ten."

Geneva leaves what she's doing and a moment later walks around front, Kyra behind her, with the newspaper in hand. It must have landed on my desk around the corner with other mail. I press it flat on the counter before me and shuffle to page ten—to see it's the obituaries.

Geneva catches that, too. "Uh oh—who died?"

I scan the few names listed and, understanding immediately why Mom texted, I announce, "Dr. Montgomery. Dr. Montgomery died."

The others gasp as Kyra says, "Oh no, he's my doctor."

"He's *everyone's* doctor," Geneva reminds her.

"Not anymore," Caroline remarks quietly.

Around seven years ago, Dr. and Mrs. Montgomery returned home to their still unsold farm and he bought back his old practice from another doctor who apparently didn't love small town medicine, either. Never a friendly man— more straightforward and all business—Dr. M. was still respected and valued in the community.

We all stay silent until Kyra asks, "How did he die?"

I scan the page and tell her, "It doesn't say. Obituaries usually don't."

"I'll text my mom," Caroline announces.

Meanwhile, assuming everyone is interested, I read the obit aloud.

It gives his age as sixty-seven, reminding me Luke's father was older than the rest of our parents—he didn't start a family until after graduating from medical school and getting professionally established.

It then touches on what a beloved member of the community he was. A strong word, *beloved*, and though none of us say that, I suspect we're all thinking it.

It goes on to list his survivors, naming his wife as well as Luke's older brothers, who now have wives and kids of their own. Both are attorneys, and I learn that one lives in Cincinnati, the other in St. Louis. The paragraph ends with the words, "and Luke Montgomery, thirty-two, of Springdale, Utah."

Okay then. He's not married with kids. But I know nothing else about him. I once casually asked Dr. Montgomery during a checkup how Luke was doing, mentioning we'd been in high school together, and all he rewarded me with was a surly, "He's fine," that made me give up the quest.

"Mom heard it was a pulmonary embolism in his sleep," Caroline interrupts me grimly to report, looking at her phone.

We all nod, then I finish the obituary by sharing the funeral date and time. "Followed by burial at the Sweetwater Cemetery."

"That's tomorrow," Caroline points out when I'm done.

"Yeah," I say, then realize they're all looking at me. "What?"

"This means Luke is in town," she says, like I haven't made that leap on my own.

I merely shrug. "So what? I haven't seen him in nearly fifteen years."

"Don't you want to? I mean, most of the town will go to the visitation, so it's only normal you would, too."

I shake my head. "I don't think so."

"Why not?"

The last time I saw him, he made me feel like dirt. Then

waltzed off into the night with Jasmine—or at least I assume he did, all things considered. I don't even like being taken back to that awful night in my memory.

Of course, much later I found out why he acted so mean. But no matter the reason, our last meeting hurt and embarrassed me. He has a life far away from here and surely won't be in Sweetwater for long. I simply offer another shrug. "It's water under the bridge."

Of course, the truth runs deeper than that, and is a little more complex.

Despite some dating along the way, I've never had much of a love life. Instead, I've thrown myself into my work. But despite the lack of romance or riches in my life, I'm happy. I make a living—however meager sometimes—doing what I love. I've actually come to appreciate my little cottage not far from the shop—I've fixed it up, painted it with fun colors inside and out, and even have a lovely flower garden in back every summer. And I've grown dedicated to supporting this town and trying to keep it alive, no matter how hard that might be getting.

So why would I want to upset my perfectly happy life by revisiting the past with Luke Montgomery?

8

JANUARY 10

Luke

Man, this place has changed. That's all I can think as I walk down a chipped sidewalk on Main Street in the town where I was raised. I've been back for holidays and my mom's birthday once or twice, but the visits have never led me into town. Not that there's much left to be led to. The place was floundering my whole life, but it seems far worse now.

Which is part of why I'm still here. I'd planned to leave right after the funeral, but more than one thing has stopped me. Mostly, it's about dealing with my father's estate and helping Mom map out a future without him. But something else has come up that makes it about the future of the entire town.

The truth is, I don't want to care very much. I haven't lived here in a long time and I have a good life in Utah. But it's my hometown. And so I guess I care.

I push through the door of the barber shop to see Stanley Ellis, who gave me my very first haircut—and now that I think about it, every haircut I had until moving away. He's gone gray since I last saw him, and looks skinnier to me as he says, "You're in need of a cut, young man. Take a seat in the chair and we'll get right to it."

He doesn't recognize me, but still thinks I need a cut. He always did. I'm not the best about keeping up with that. It makes me smile as I tell him, "It's me, Stan. Luke Montgomery."

The older man's eyes widen on me. "Well, good gravy, Luke, I didn't realize." Then his expression goes somber. "Was real sorry to hear about your pop."

I give the same nod I've been giving for days now. "Thanks, Stan." I leave it at that. I should be more emotional about it, I know. Instead, it's only made me feel kind of empty inside. "But I'm not here for a trim."

He gives his head a judgmental tilt. "Maybe you should be."

I just laugh. "Another day soon."

Then his silvery eyebrows shoot up. "You stayin' in town?"

"For a little while. To help settle Dad's affairs and deal with some business for Mom."

"That's good of you," he says. "She's a sweet woman, your mama."

Everyone says that. Some people wonder how she ended

up with Dad. She was always happy with him, though—she might be the one person in the world he had a soft spot for. "She is," I agree.

Then I get to the reason I'm here, reaching in the folder I'm carrying to pull out a flyer. "Listen, I want to invite you to a meeting. Something's come up, an offer on our property, that will affect all of Sweetwater, and I want to get input from the remaining business owners."

As he takes the flyer I hold out, his brow knits. "What sorta offer could affect us *here*? Your farm's a good mile or so away."

All I tell him is, "It's not really that far when you think about it. But I don't want to get into specifics until everyone is gathered together. Hope you'll come."

Now he's studying the sheet of paper in his hand. "Oh, I'll be there," he says. I can see I've made him worry, which isn't my intent. Or...maybe he *should* worry. All depends on how you look at it.

As I make my way back toward the door of his old shop, he calls, "And you get back in here for that haircut."

I promise I will, and I mean it, not because I want the cut so much as I can see the guy needs the business.

When I stop into the deli next door—a newer establishment—I'm told the owner is away on an errand right now, but the older woman behind the counter promises to deliver the flyer. It's just past noon and I'm glad to see that *this* business at least has a few patrons, and I decide to add to that by ordering an egg salad sandwich, which I eat with chips at one of the little two-seat tables lining the front window.

Afterward, I cross the street to the diner from my youth. As I push through the plate-glass door, it seems brighter than I remember, with a few people seated at booths and tables.

But then I spot something that jolts me—and I'm unexpectedly transported back in time, in ways both good and bad. A memorable wooden heart-shaped box sits on the counter. It was white the last time I saw it, but now it's pink. Damn, I can't believe she's still here.

"Can I help you?" a pony-tailed girl asks in greeting.

I can't hold in my smile as I gesture toward the wooden box. "I'd know that box anywhere," I tell her. "Is Taylor Mulvaney here?"

"She owns the place," the girl informs me, "but she's away right now."

Despite myself, I'm disappointed. When last we met, it was in the face of a rejection that wounded me more than I could have anticipated—but that was a long time ago, and it would be nice to say hi. "I went to school with her," I tell the clerk. "She had that box as far back as elementary school. Her dad made it for her, and she'd bring it on Valentine's Day when we all traded cards." I'm not sure why I'm telling her all this, but maybe I'm still absorbing my surprise at finding out Taylor's still in Sweetwater—and *owns* this place?

"Oh, I didn't know that," the girl says, sounding interested. "Now people put their business cards in and Taylor draws one out to win a cake or pie every week."

The wheels of my brain are turning. "She only goes through it weekly, huh?"

I'm happily surprised when the young girl shrugs and

tells me, "Actually, she takes a peek inside every day or two. Once someone thought it would be a good idea to place an order for ten pies by dropping a note in the box without telling anyone, and chaos ensued. So she checks for anything that's not a business card like clockwork."

"If I put something in, think you could make sure she sees it today?" Yeah, I could just hand the flyer to the clerk, but guess the sight of this box has me reminiscent.

"Absolutely," she promises.

Of course, the last thing I dropped in it, back in high school, didn't exactly have the desired effect, but even so, I wish I could see the look on Taylor's face when she finds this. Will it take her back to a time when we were friends? Or maybe it'll be more like: *Ugh, him again.* I never really understood why she blatantly ignored my invitation altogether, but we were just kids. And either way, it'll give her a blast from the past.

Pulling one of the flyers from my folder, I reach for a pen on the counter and write a note at the top:

I remember this box almost as well as I remember my old friend, the keeper of the heart wishes. Luke

Then I fold the 8x10 sheet of paper a few times and slip it through the slot, an act that feels strangely familiar even after all these years.

Exiting the diner, my mind stays on the girl I used to know. I thought she hated Sweetwater and assumed she'd be long gone by now. I'm even more shocked to discover she bought a business in this doomed little town. Or...maybe she's married and shares it with her significant other. Maybe it's about family being here, or any number of other possibilities. I wonder if she still has that fiery red hair. Those curls seemed almost untamable at times, but I thought it was amazing. She always looked a little windblown—in a way I liked.

I hope she accepts *this* invitation—not only for the sake of her business, but because now that I know she's in Sweetwater, I can't leave town without seeing her again.

Taylor

I'm heading back from Sweetwater Drugs—where I took a surprise heart cake to the owner, Jeff Calloway, since today is his fortieth birthday. Everyone there—which was me, one employee, and one customer—sang happy birthday while he blew out the candles I stuck on top.

It's cold but sunny, I'm having Caroline over for pizza and a movie tonight, and all feels right with the world—until I approach the bake shop, reach to open the door, and see none other than Luke Montgomery standing inside.

My heart nearly stops. How can this be? And why is he still so incredible looking?

Somehow, all this time, I've pictured him in that cowboy hat and beard—maybe because it's the last image I had of him from pictures Jasmine posted—but in fact, he's clean-shaven if still a little in need of a trim, and he's aged like a fine wine. Well, better than a fine wine in my opinion, because I don't really know wine, but I know that Luke Montgomery looks good enough to eat.

I've stopped outside, peering through the plate-glass door

of my shop like a thief deciding my next move, and when it appears he's getting ready to leave, I panic. Even more, since I'm *already* pretty panicked. I turn back the way I came, darting up the sidewalk until I reach the narrow alley between my building and the next, a passage just wide enough for the garbage cans tucked away there.

On pure instinct, I plaster myself against the old brick wall, trying to make myself invisible to any passersby. Well, mainly *one* passerby, who may or may not pass by.

That's when Caroline approaches from the opposite direction and stops, squinting at me like she's seen a ghost. "What are you doing?" The ghost of an idiot perhaps, because clearly my plan isn't working.

Even so, I grab her wrist and pull her into hiding with me —a term I use loosely here. "Stay out of sight," I whisper, then make the daring move to peek around the corner toward my own front door. It's open and he's exiting.

I re-plaster myself to the wall and motion for her to do the same. She's looking at me like I'm crazy, understandably, but follows suit anyway. Which is a great example of why I love her.

"Shhh," I say, my skin prickling as footsteps grow near.

Please don't let him find us because this was dumb of me and I have no way to explain it other than I really am as weird as people thought in school. Or maybe, more accurately, they *turned* me weird. But that hardly matters right now.

I can barely breathe as this hot, handsome, grown-up version of my high school crush walks past. My chest tightens and my skin tingles in the cold air.

Caroline and I both stay silent and still as he moves

farther up the sidewalk. Only once we've concluded that he's gone into the drugstore does Caroline say very calmly, "That was Luke Montgomery."

"It was," I confirm.

"And you were hiding from him."

"Correct."

"Very mature."

"Agreed."

"Was he in your shop?"

I nod, then explain how I almost ran into him but didn't. "I just...wasn't mentally prepared, you know? I've been baking all morning and probably look awful."

She tilts her head, giving me a once over, then reaches up to brush something from the curls next to my face. "You do have a little flour in your hair."

I sigh. "Of course I do. And normally I don't care about things like that—I just took Jeff a cake and obviously didn't care enough to check a mirror first. But if I'm gonna see Luke for the first time since high school, with flour in my hair is not how I want to do it."

She purses her full lips. "So you *do* plan on seeing him while he's here."

I shake my head. "No. What are you talking about? I don't even know how long he's in town. I just meant if I *were* going to. But I'm not."

"I wonder how long he's staying." She pulls out her phone. "I'll text my mom."

After she hits Send, she looks back at me. "You really should connect with him. For old time's sake."

"I'd rather not."

"Why? After all, your last communication from him was a nice invitation to a dance."

"Correction. My last communication with him was him being snarly because he didn't know I never got it. And..." I think it through. "I guess what it really comes down to, though, is...in some moments, I'm still that paranoid girl who doesn't feel good enough because everyone *treated me* like I wasn't good enough."

At this, my longtime bestie lets out an understanding sigh. "Look," she says, "I, more than anyone, get it. But you need to let that go. And honestly, I thought you had. You float through life with ease now, perfectly happy."

"Until I'm confronted with the past," I confess. "Then I'm dragged back there in my mind. It's easy to be confident when everything's going fine and people treat you kindly. But those reminders of worse days are hard."

When her phone buzzes, she looks down and tells me, "Mom doesn't know why he's still here or for how long, darn it." She shakes her head, appearing put out. "My top gossip source has let me down."

"Nobody's perfect, I guess."

A little while later, as I help Kyra box up some online orders for a post office run, Luke is still on my mind. Oh, who am I kidding? He's been there all week, ever since I found out about his dad's death, but now it's worse. Because now I've seen how good he still looks. And I'm a little more mired in wishing things had been different with him in the past.

"Before I forget," Kyra tells me, "you need to check your heart box."

My hand goes still on my tongs. Normally, this would have me asking her questions about why, but knowing who was just here a little while ago, I don't bother. I just abandon the order, go to the counter, and take off the lid, happy the shop is empty right now other than her. Inside, on top, I find a folded sheet of paper, which I open and read.

***Calling all Sweetwater business owners!
Come to a special meeting about Sweetwater's
future!
Sweetwater High School gym
January 12, 7:00 P.M.***

An opportunity has been presented to my family that would have a significant impact on all of Sweetwater. Your attendance is important and your feedback valued. I apologize for being mysterious, but this will be better discussed in person, as a group. Thanks in advance.

Luke Montgomery

It's a baffling invitation, to be sure, but what my eyes stay stuck on is the note from him, to me, at the top. He called me the keeper of the heart wishes once before, that day so long ago outside the lunchroom, the day he dropped an invitation in the valentine box that I didn't see for four years. I always remembered because I liked the idea—of being the keeper of heart wishes. I'm amazed he remembers it, too.

That's when my phone buzzes with a text from Caroline across the street. *Did you get your invitation to a mysterious meeting?*

I reply. *Yep.*

Going?

I hesitate before answering. I *could* just get scoop from Caroline.

But that's when Maggie lets out a little bark, and I glance down to see a clump of her thick, wintertime fur has smushed itself into the shape of a heart. My eyes pick it out immediately, same as always since losing my dad nearly twenty years ago.

I release a long sigh. Hearts in unusual places have continued to be guideposts for me. And Caroline's right—I need to be mature and face my past. Hiding in the alleyway a little while ago was not my finest moment.

I guess I'm just remembering...how long it took to get over him back in the day. Maybe it was more than a crush I had. I didn't know him *well*, but I knew him for a long time—I let those feelings grow and evolve inside me for eight long years. And perhaps I'm afraid seeing him will bring back up emotions I worked long and hard to move past.

But on the bright side, at least I can control this encounter. I'm still the girl with red hair and freckles, but at least I can make sure there's no flour in the equation. I can walk in strong and confident and ready. I can walk in basically being...me. The me I've grown into.

And sure, sometimes I really *am* the girl with flour in her hair, too—but I don't need to show him that part.

Yes, I'll go, I finally text back.

Good, Caroline answers. *It'll be fine, you'll see.*

I have no idea if that's true. But despite what I told her in the alley, like it or not, sounds like I'm seeing Luke Montgomery again.

9

JANUARY 12

Taylor

Caroline and I ride together to the big meeting. We still have no idea what it could be about despite all the conjecture put forth between us, us being Geneva, Kyra, Jeff, barber Stan, Caroline's mother—and even Billy Finch, another of Luke's old friends, who owns a car repair shop on the edge of town. We were all sure Billy would know, but when Jeff called him to ask, he said that other than going to Dr. M's funeral, he hadn't talked to Luke since high school.

Walking back into the school that holds so many memories feels weird, but I push it down as we enter the gym. People mill about in front of the old bleachers where I once sat to watch Luke play basketball.

Then I spot Luke himself talking with his old pals, TJ and Billy. My chest tightens, but I'm not sure if that's because he's so good-looking or because I'm a little nervous, even *with* the advance warning. He's in casual khakis and a cozy-looking half-zip pullover, a dark T-shirt peeking out from underneath. I'm guessing TJ might have helped secure the gym for tonight.

Me, I'm in today's pink *Sweetwater Bake Shop (Not a Diner!)* shirt because Caroline and I came straight from work, where I left Geneva baking cookies and ready to greet any late day customers, even though we don't get many after dark in the winter until closer to Valentine's Day. I considered changing into something nicer, but flour in hair notwithstanding, I decided to just be me. Because I've made too much of this. He's going to talk, and I'm going to think he's handsome, and we're going to say hi afterward and do a three-minute catch-up, and then life will go on. And probably the much bigger headline from the evening will be whatever this mystery opportunity turns out to be.

By meeting time, only a couple dozen of us are gathered, and it makes me sad to realize this is how few independently-owned businesses still exist in Sweetwater, on or away from Main Street. I'm also sorry to look up and see Jasmine walk in with her mother. As before, she's dressed like she's going to some ritzy soiree, today in a form-fitting black-and-white dress worthy of a fashion magazine, rather than to a high school gymnasium.

Caroline and I exchange looks just before I see my one-time tormenter lift a small wave in Luke's direction. My stomach churns with the knowledge that she knows him so much better than I do, that she's had so much more with him than I ever will. But maybe that's why I *didn't* overdress for the occasion—I'm just keeping things real, just on hand to hear the big announcement.

With Caroline, Jasmine, TJ, Billy, and of course, Luke all here, it feels like a surreal class reunion I would never want to go to. So I'm glad when everyone is seated and Luke starts the meeting.

"Thank you all for coming." His voice is deeper than in high school, rugged and masculine-sounding, and despite my best intentions, it reverberates deep into my solar plexus. Maybe I'm not as in control here as I thought.

"As I said on the flyer, I apologize for being vague, but—" That's when his voice cuts off and I realize he's looking at... me. Like maybe he just now saw me. He fumbles over his words a little before getting back on track. "But..." He clears his throat. "But I think you'll understand why a meeting felt like the best, most useful way to share this news." I try to ignore his verbal stumble and not wonder what it means.

As he goes on, he seems to direct his glance elsewhere. And that bugs me—because am I so awful to look at? Or...am I just imagining it, because this whole event is whisking me back to a different place in time? I work to refocus on what he's saying, though I've already missed some of it.

"You all know Hank, proprietor of the Sweetwater Inn." He motions to graying, fifty-something Hank below me on the bleachers, who lifts his hand in a non-smiling wave. "Hank and my family have been approached jointly with an offer from the Northcutt Drywall Manufacturing Company to buy our riverfront property." The inn's land connects to the Montgomery farm. And this news perks my ears up as tension suddenly blankets the air.

"They'd like to build a factory on our land to utilize the gypsum that's a byproduct of the coal-burning power plants up the river. Apparently each plant produces a bargeful every day. The structure they want to erect would be enormous—a million square feet, which we're told is approximately twenty-eight footfall fields.

"Obviously, we're talking about a lot of money here. But we're also talking about changing the face of Sweetwater. As you all know, Hank's property goes all the way into town, butting up against the old park behind Main Street. If the plant is built, much of the town's river view would become obscured by a huge industrial compound several stories high."

Palpable groans echo through the small crowd before Luke goes on. "This is why Mom and I decided it was only fair to talk to community business owners before we make a decision, since it would affect you the most. But," he goes on, holding up one finger, "I have to point out the flip side of losing the view, as well. That flip side is significant. New jobs. New housing. A new influx of residents. It's no secret that Sweetwater is dying, that people continue to leave and Main Street grows more desolate every year. I can't predict the future, but I believe this would change that. I believe some—and maybe all—of those empty storefronts would get filled.

"If you're wondering what my mother's wishes are now that she's on her own...well, it's early days for her in that regard, but she's open-minded. She's happy on the farm, but she feels she could be happy elsewhere, too. And so, with that, I'll open it up for discussion."

Instead of discussion, though, a bunch of muttering and grumbling quickly fills the gym. Luke raises his voice above it to say, "Look, I know I've opened a huge can of worms here. I get it. If you want to yell, yell. If you want to cuss, cuss. But I'm hoping we can all stay calm and have a productive conversation."

That's when Billy, still in his work shirt and a Finch Auto Repair ball cap, throws up his hand to weigh in, bluntly, "Since you're asking, Luke, I say no. Who wants to live in a place where we're walled off from the river by a factory? Sounds ugly as hell."

"But we gotta look at it from both angles," Jeff insists, shoving wire-rimmed glasses up his nose. "This could keep a lot of us in business who are struggling every day."

"I agree," says Mary Beth McClain, who owns a tire company with her husband. "More people means more cars. Good for us and you both, Billy."

"But this is Sweetwater," declares Amy Holcumb, who runs the Little Dipper Dairy Bar just outside town with her parents. "Sweetwater isn't gonna be very sweet anymore with no view of the water. And it sounds like this giant plant would block *our* view at the Dipper, too. We don't have much in this town, but we have our river and our view. People come out to get ice cream on summer nights and sit at our picnic tables to watch the water roll by as the sun sets. You might say it'll bring more people, but the Little Dipper would be ruined." The dark hair falling in thick waves around her face somehow only serves to make her appear even more sullen.

After a few people chime in agreeing with her, Luke acknowledges, "No getting around the fact that it'll affect some more than others."

And then Hank speaks up. "For what it's worth, I told the Northcutt people I'd sell in a heartbeat. You know how many rooms I got occupied at the inn right now? Zero. If not for the few weddings and parties we get, I'd have closed my doors years ago. And it's getting worse all the time. For me, this would be an answer to a prayer, an easy retirement, college tuition for my grandkids. Without it, bankruptcy could be a month or two away at any given moment. Only problem I got is they don't want my place if they can't have Luke's, too." He stops, sighs. "Of course, I'll survive whatever's decided. And I feel bad for folks it might hurt more than it helps. But I gotta look out for myself as well."

Sitting there taking all this in—and it's a lot—I can see both sides. Would I love a more vibrant Main Street? Of course. And even with my online business, I struggle to make ends meet on a regular basis, trying to make February profits stretch through the rest of the year. But do I think some behemoth factory right on the river is the right answer for Sweetwater? It's almost unimaginable. I'm pretty sure my own house, a few blocks up from the park, would sit in its shadow. My whole neighborhood would, in fact.

Talk goes on for another half hour or so, and Luke answers questions about the proposed situation as best he can. Finally, Jasmine's mom, Janet, always smartly put together in a blazer and tailored skirt, asks, "What do you think you'll do, Luke?"

The weight of everyone's opposing concerns is etched on

his handsome face. Finally, he says, "I'm not sure. I'd hoped maybe I'd leave this meeting feeling clearer on an answer, but instead the opposite is true."

"Whatever you decide, it's real decent of you and your mom to take us into consideration," Mary Beth remarks.

Others murmur their agreement, but it's easy to see how upset people are. I'm among them, but I'm not even sure what I'm rooting for. Build it and Sweetwater loses its only remaining bit of charm, turning it ugly and uninviting, cutting it off from its namesake—the water that lines its shore. Don't build it and more of us continue to lose our livelihoods.

"All I can tell you," Luke finally says, "is that I take all your concerns very seriously, and Mom and I will talk more about it."

"Where do your brothers stand on the issue?" Billy asks then.

"They want to sell," Luke tells him.

"Easy for them to say," Billy murmurs. "They don't live here anymore."

To which Luke replies, "Exactly. That's why I wanted to talk to the people who do. And to be completely transparent, Northcutt wants an answer by the end of the month. I'll let you all know what we decide as soon as possible."

As people begin to stand up, most looking a little shell-shocked, it occurs to me that Luke doesn't live here, either, but was still kind enough to be concerned and not just take the money and run. It's surely enough to leave his whole family set for life.

That's when Caroline nudges me. "You should go say hi."

"Oh. Right." I should. I'm just still trying to absorb this news.

As we reach the gym floor, I take a deep breath and start toward him—which is when Jasmine rushes up from where she sat in the front row, takes both his hands in hers, then leans in close to whisper something.

I pull up short, then switch my gaze to Caroline. "That's my cue to leave."

Caroline practically snarls in response. "Like I said, this town was a nicer place without her."

All of us look like a bunch of zombies as we wander out into the parking lot, no one speaking. Again, the shock runs thick.

But once in Caroline's car, the two of us sit and talk a while, debating the pros and cons of the situation. We waffle back and forth between imagining the possibilities for a Sweetwater that has a sudden growth in population and lamenting that no matter how many people come and how much business it brings, what remains of our small town ambience would be destroyed.

As Caroline drives me back to the bake shop to relieve Geneva, get the dog, and close up, I finally conclude, "I guess I'm just glad I'm not the one who has to make this decision."

When I open the shop's front door, Geneva meets me at it, coat in hand. "Sorry to rush out, hon, but Leslie got called in to the hospital and needs me to babysit."

My eyes go wide. "Oh no—I'm sorry to hold you up. Get going." I shoo her off to help her daughter, and she starts up the sidewalk—but then stops and looks back, her eyes going wide. "I almost forgot. You have a customer."

I blink, surprised. People use the booths and tables some during the day, but at nighttime—and in January, no less—it's almost unheard of. "Oh. Okay." Then I shoo her again and step inside.

Whipping off my winter scarf, I loop it over a hook just inside the door, then bend to pet the Magster. Only upon rising back up do I spot a man in the back booth, facing me—and that's when I understand Geneva's wide gaze. Luke Montgomery pins me in place with his blue, blue eyes.

"If it's not Taylor Mulvaney," he says, flashing a small smile, "keeper of the heart wishes."

Maybe I liked that better in writing. Here, now, it makes me feel more like that insecure girl who sat outside the cafeteria than the grown woman I am now. Like someone who collected *other* people's wishes, too frightened to harbor any of her own. "Not anymore," I tell him quietly. "That was a long time ago."

He shrugs, as if weighing my words. "In some ways, it feels like yesterday."

Not caring to explore that—because I like my *now* better than I liked my *then*—I drop my glance to the half-eaten heart-shaped treat on a plate in front of him. "How's your cupcake?"

Offering up a slow, nostalgic smile, he says, "Word of the day: *Delicious*." Then adds a small laugh. "But not exactly a very highbrow word of the day, huh? Could be my vocabulary quit expanding after I left home."

I only shrug. "Maybe it makes more sense for the word of

the day to be what the day, or the moment, is about more than being an impressive word."

He gives an agreeable nod. "Fair enough." Then tilts that handsome head of his. "Though I actually came in for a burger and fries because I forgot it's—"

"Not a diner," I finish for him, pointing at the slogan on my shirt. "Yeah, that's a common mistake around here. The diner couldn't stay in business when it was a diner—now that it's not a diner, everyone wants a diner."

"But you do well with the place, I hope?" His eyebrows rise, awaiting my answer.

And I want to lie, claiming wild success. I want him to think I'm having an incredible life. But the truth is all around us, in the empty shop on an empty street in an empty town. So I merely shrug. "Well, I'm solvent—because a lot of my sales are online. They kinda have to be around here. And if things get any worse, it could easily do us in."

"I guess all that could change if the drywall company comes."

"Maybe," I reply, keeping it simple. "Meanwhile, my busy season is just around the corner. Everybody wants heart-shaped baked goods on Valentine's Day."

Grinning, he motions toward the counter. "I recognized the box."

"Ah, the memories." He has no idea how long I've actually associated the valentine box with *him*. All the way back to that day he defended my honor in the fourth grade. I'm suddenly tempted to explain why I didn't show at the sweetheart dance when we were seniors, but it seems almost childish to bring it up. What if he doesn't even remember?

Unlike me, he probably hasn't spent all these years thinking about it.

After taking another bite, he says, "I remember you running that baking club in high school."

I nod. "It became a lifelong passion." *Kind of like* you.

But what am I thinking? I don't even know him anymore, and I barely did then. All I really knew was that he chose to be nice to me. And all I really know now is that he's hot. So hot that I'm pretty proud of myself for not tripping all over my words or acting weird as I talk to him. Compared to how I feel inside, I think I'm coming off pretty cool.

And I want to ask him a million things in this moment. Why did you go to Utah? What do you do there? Do you have a girlfriend? Are you happy? But I don't. Because there remains this proud part of me that doesn't want to act like I care. Despite him asking me to that dance, I'm the one who had the years-long crush—and I simply want to be above all that now. Even if it's only pretend.

Almost as if he senses me holding back, and thinks it means I want him to leave, he stands up. "I should let you be on your way. But thanks for the cupcake."

"Of course," I say as he starts past me toward the door. "And...thanks for taking all of us into account before you make your decision."

He stops and looks back. "What's *your* vote?"

I let out a sigh. "Undecided. It's a tough call, with pros and cons on both sides."

He just nods, turns to go, and says, "Goodnight, Taylor," with one last glance back at me.

"Goodnight, Luke."

As the door shuts behind him, I feel like I can breathe again, like maybe I haven't breathed normally since finding him in my back booth. The same booth where I once sat watching him kiss Jasmine Dupree after he sneered at me.

Only...what was he actually doing here? Really seeking a burger?

Or did he come for something else? After all, he knew I owned the place. Is it possible he was looking for *me* more than something to eat?

That's when I notice a patch of frost on the window—loosely in the shape of a heart. Oh, geez, a message from above—now?

With no time to think, I step outside and look around, quickly spotting the one lone person on Main Street walking toward a big, black SUV—which I think belonged to his father—parked along the curb. "Hey," I call.

He looks back. I can't make out his expression in the dark.

"If you're hungry, they still serve hamburgers at the Little Dipper. Open until nine most nights."

"Thanks," he says. "I'll try them." Then he tilts his head. "Have you eaten?"

"Um...no, actually."

"Care to join?"

I hesitate only briefly. "Sure—I could go for a burger," I say as if it hadn't crossed my mind. Joining him was actually my whole half-baked plan when I came barreling out the door, but I didn't deliver that part accurately, flying by the seat of my pants and all. Thank God he asked. "Let me close up and I'll be five minutes behind you."

Stepping back inside, I lock the front door, grab Maggie, and head out back to where I park.

A few minutes later, I'm taking my dog inside the house and flipping on a light. "Hold down the fort until I get home, Mags, and wish me luck." Scratching her sweet little head, I add, "I only hope I don't regret this."

The good news: Luke's announcement in the gym didn't send Amy and her parents into a closing-up-early tailspin—they're happy to cook us up some burgers and fries.

The bad: Amy's dad, Paul, grills Luke about the situation while we wait, so much that it begins to feel contentious, and I'm aware the whole time that it's my fault he's here.

When finally we're sitting across from each other in one of the aging red booths that line the front of the old-fashioned drive-in restaurant, a tray full of food between us, I say, "I hope you don't end up wishing you hadn't included us all in your decision."

But he shakes his head before he bites into his hamburger. "No, it felt like the right thing to do—and I knew it would be upsetting to some. I can take it."

It occurs to me then that maybe he's had a lot to "take," lately, and I haven't even acknowledged the big loss in his life. "By the way, I'm sorry about your dad."

Peeking up at me from beneath lowered eyelids, he nods, his mouth full.

"I'm sure it came as a shock."

Another nod, followed by, "It's been hard on my mom."

Not you, too? I don't ask, though—it's none of my business. Instead, I say, "Good of you to stay and help her get this big piece of business handled. Do you expect to be in town long?"

"Big business, little business—there's a lot to settle, from my dad's medical practice to getting everything put in my mom's name. And neither of my brothers seem willing to help much, so that leaves me." He sighs. "Not that I'm complaining. They have families, and I'm single—so I get it. Sort of, anyway. I'll be here a few weeks—or more, I guess—until we get things ironed out. Then back to Utah."

Okay—the obituary made it clear he didn't have a wife, but sounds like there's also no significant other. One big question answered. And finally, an opening to ask something else I've wondered all these years. "How on earth did you end up in Utah, Luke Montgomery?"

He tips his head back in a small laugh that tells me he's probably been asked this a lot since coming back to Sweetwater. "A guy I knew in college invited me out there for the summer after my junior year. He'd arranged a job on a horse ranch and got me on, too. I missed having horses, so it sounded like a good way to spend the time, and a good reason not to go home to my parents' place in Cincinnati, since Dad and I weren't getting along too well.

"Long story short, I loved the work so much that I dropped out of school and stayed." He rolls his eyes as he blows out a breath. "Man, were Mom and Dad pissed. And I get it. But I'd been following *their* dream for me, not mine."

"And then what?" I ask, munching on a fry as I await his answer.

"The ranch wasn't far from Zion National Park, and I got into hiking and exploring the area. It's really beautiful out there—a mind-blowing view around every corner. As much as I loved the ranch job, it didn't pay much, so after a couple years, I started working for an outfitter. It's the kind of place that rents hiking equipment and mountain bikes—but I mostly took people on tours and guided hikes.

"Eventually, my boss was ready to retire," he goes on, "so I bought the place. I never saw myself as a business owner, but I'd gotten close to the guy and he really wanted me to take over, so I got a small business loan and it's gone well. I live in Springdale, a cute little tourist town just outside Zion, but a few years ago I opened a second location in Moab, near Arches and Canyonlands, so I go back and forth between the two a lot."

I smile as certain things start making more sense to me now. That cowboy hat, for one. And for another, "Now I get it. Why you felt compelled to tell us all about the drywall company. You're a small business owner, too."

He tilts his head, looking enlightened. "That actually hadn't even hit me," he says on a laugh. "But yeah, maybe that played into it. Speaking of which…"

"Yeah?" I ask, dipping another fry into ketchup.

"You bought the old diner, huh? I didn't see that coming."

"Neither did I," I confess. "But when Walt offered me the place dirt cheap, I followed my own little dream—of opening a bake shop."

"Hey now," he chides me, pointing his own fry in my direction, "no dream is little. In fact, taking on a business is huge. Trust me, I know."

We're smiling at each other now and I'm liking that we actually have something in common after all those years when we didn't.

"And I'm glad you still have that heart-shaped box of yours," he adds. "Seeing it when I came in the other day took me back in time."

My breath catches a little, for many reasons, not the least of which is...finding out that maybe *he* reminisces, too. That maybe something about the box, or dare I think *me*, meant something to him once upon a time. Even if it was just a *little* something, it's still nice.

And so, despite deciding against it earlier, I make the split-second decision to tell him. "Speaking of the valentine box...I, uh, found something inside it a few years after high school that had gotten stuck in some gluey stuff on the lid."

His eyes narrow in confusion until I conclude he has no idea what I'm talking about.

So I have no choice but to spell it out. "Your invitation to the sweetheart dance."

The look in his blue eyes changes from bewilderment to understanding. "Oh. Wow." But then his brow knits. "It got... stuck?"

I nod. "Sounds weird, I know. But the inside of the box had gotten decoupaged the night before I was selling those wishes, and I just never looked under the lid until years later."

"That's...crazy."

Even now, I can't fully read his expression, and I have no idea how much he recalls about that time or how much it mattered to him—or not. But I finish my confession with,

"And for the record, I would have come." Though my heart starts beating harder as I say it. This has suddenly gone from small talk over burgers to admitting: *I once felt something romantic for you.*

"For the record," he replies, "I had flowers and everything."

It's all I can do not to gasp. He *does* remember. And he had flowers. For me. My breath goes shallow as I tell him, "For the record, I'm really sorry I missed that. I...didn't get much of that in high school." As in any.

He leans a little closer over the table. "For the record, you should have. And it was gonna be a great night."

Again, I struggle to catch my breath. And now I've stopped being strategic—I'm just saying what comes naturally. "For the record, I...never thought you liked me. *That* way."

"For the record, I did," he goes on. "I'm just sorry it took me so long to realize it. But I totally did."

Well, that's it. Now I *really* can't breathe. But I don't want him to see that. So I don't respond right away, stuck for words now, trying to inhale and exhale normally. Finally, what I come up with is, "I'm sorry. That I didn't see your note."

"No, *I'm* sorry. I was a kid and it was a stupid way to ask you out."

"Not so stupid," I absolve him. "The box is special to me, so I like the idea of being asked that way."

"If only it had actually worked. Instead..." He makes a face.

And I'm back to not knowing what he's thinking, but I

know what *I'm* remembering. So I roll with it. "Instead you were mad at me."

He lets out a sigh. "Immature, I know." His gaze narrows and he leans forward as if about to confide in me. "Guess I've never handled rejection very well." He gives his head a short shake and keeps going. "Anyway, I'm sorry about that. Sorry about a lot of things. Because if I'd been smart enough to just ask you if you'd gotten the note, maybe things would have been different."

"Different how?" I bravely venture.

He shrugs his shoulders. "Who can say? But for starters, I wouldn't have felt so on the rebound that I ended up with Jasmine." He rolls his eyes, then adds, looking almost embarrassed, "I don't know if you know this, but...I actually had a long-term relationship with her. From the end of high school until about a year after I moved out west."

I'm proud of how casual my response sounds. "Yeah, I think I heard that somewhere." *Not that I obsessed over it or anything. Not that images she posted of the two of you together burned themselves into my brain.*

"Not my best move," he says. "In the end, it was definitely a mistake."

I, of course, want to ask why and how and what happened. Again, I want to ask a *million* questions, about his father's death and rejection and more about his life in Utah. But my head is spinning with an almost overpowering attraction that has me feeling awkward and nervous despite that I'm hiding it well. So all I say in reply is, "We all make 'em sometimes."

He lifts his gaze to mine again. "I hope whatever Mom and I decide about the drywall factory isn't one. A mistake."

I find myself trying to think hopefully, in some new direction. "Maybe there's an answer that makes sense for everyone. Something that just hasn't come to you yet."

"I doubt that." He sounds skeptical—but then admits, "Though until right now, it hadn't even occurred to me there might be anything besides the 'either' 'or' of it. The 'yes' or the 'no.' And maybe there isn't. But I'll at least think about it a while before giving the place an answer."

A few minutes later, as we're standing up to put on our coats, he comes back to the topic, sounding melancholy. "It's hard to imagine letting them plow the farm under—the house, the barn, all of it."

"I've always thought it looked beautiful driving by," I say.

He squints. "You've never been there?"

I just laugh. "When would I have been there? I wasn't part of your *friend group*, remember?" I use the same old air quotes.

He laughs, too, if a bit cynically. "You're right—and I deserve that." Then he glances in the direction of the farm, not far up the road from the Little Dipper. "You should come see it while I'm here. In case it's gone soon."

"That sounds nice," I answer as we step out into the cold night air.

Directly across from us stands the once-pristine, now-worn sign for the Sweetwater Inn. It marks a winding drive that leads across gently sloped grounds stretching from the road toward the riverbank, eventually reaching the historic white-columned building. Across the wide-open space dotted with clumps of pine trees, I catch the sparkle of moonlight on the big river in the distance.

"This *is* a nice spot to sit with a cone on a summer night," I muse.

He looks around, taking it in. "You're right, it is."

After we exchange numbers, he tells me he'll be in touch about giving me that farm tour and says, "It's really good to see you again, Taylor."

"You too, Luke," I reply, cool as a cucumber.

Though once I'm shut safely and privately into the dark interior of my car, I'm almost swept back to being a teenager again, reeling with the romance of it all.

But...is that what this catch-up session and farm invite is? Romance? Or is it just friendship? And am I still too naïve to tell the difference?

The only thing I know for sure is that I must, must, must keep this in perspective and not let myself be that teenager again. Yes, my schoolgirl crush is suddenly back in my life in a better way than he ever was before. But he has a whole separate existence far away from Sweetwater, and in the end, this will be over before I can even blink and find a heart in the clouds.

10

JANUARY 15

Luke

Plopping a favorite old straw cowboy hat on my head, I step out of the one-time carriage house—which now serves as an office and guesthouse—behind my family's big Victorian home.

After breakfast with Mom next to a big picture window that looks out on the river, I spent the morning in the office making phone calls to lawyers, insurance companies, and banks. My eldest brother, Tom, was named the executor in my father's will, but he pushily renounced the position to me after declaring before the funeral that there was "no way I can leave my clients and family for that long without warning." He and Aaron both have a history of acting like running *my* business couldn't possibly be as serious an endeavor as running theirs.

Thank God I have good people and reliable systems in place at Canyon Life Outfitters—I check in to both locations daily, and other than having to put out a few small fires via email and make a couple of executive decisions over the phone, things have run smoothly. Not because it's a simple business, but because my predecessor taught me how to operate it well.

The day is sunny and clear, and though patches of snow dot the ground from a snowfall a couple of nights ago, temps are warming into the forties this afternoon, making it a nice day for Taylor's visit.

As I stride toward the horse barn in cowboy boots, I feel deep down inside how good it was to see her again. And damn, she's even prettier than I remembered. Still with the wild hair and freckles, the bright eyes and smile that lights up a room. Or a diner in this case. Well, wait—not a diner, a bake shop. I laugh to myself, remembering her t-shirt. I'm glad she's coming over. It's been a hard visit home for all the obvious reasons—and she's turned into an unexpected bright spot.

Another bright spot? The horses. As I step into the barn, the smells of hay and equines relax me the way the scent of lavender does other people. Since returning to Sweetwater, Mom and Dad have had a local couple on hire who come care for the horses daily, but I'm enjoying pitching in with that, and even gave them the day off today.

As a gray appaloosa named Ash pokes his head from his stable to greet me, I take up a hard-bristled brush and smooth it over his neck. Ash is older and not saddle-broken, but he and I have bonded since my arrival home.

"Hey buddy," I say, "how ya doin'? How's that hoof?" Normally by this time of day, all our horses would be out in the pastures that stretch between the road and the river, but I've held two back to ride today, along with Ash—he lost a shoe yesterday and the farrier is due this afternoon. "We'll get you fixed up and good as new."

Horses calm me. Maybe I even forgot how much until getting to commune with them since coming home. Although I'm not sure I ever admitted it to myself, I think when Dad moved us to Cincinnati, I was as upset about selling our horses as I was leaving school.

And given the gravity of the decision before me, I *need* some calm. Part of me wishes that drywall company had never found our little stretch of prime, flat riverfront property. But when Mom told me that Dad, along with Hank, had already agreed to meet with their representatives, I figured we should hear what they had to say. And after that, I figured we should think about who it might help versus who it might hurt.

But damn, it's a complicated thing to have hanging over my head along with all the other aspects of settling my father's affairs. The end of the month is coming fast and we're not any closer to an answer than we were the day we met with them.

Feeling my blood pressure begin to rise, I step over to the next stall where a big, white gentle giant stands, ready for a nose scratch, which I gladly supply. "Hey there, Sandy, old pal. Gonna take you and Sugar out today. Ready to get saddled up?"

Of course, Sandy doesn't answer, but talking to them has come naturally to me as long as I can remember. Even if they're not talking back, it's always felt like real communication on some level.

I haven't ridden in a while—life's been getting in the way—but when you've done it enough, riding a horse is like riding a bike. The softness of the wool saddle blanket in my hands and the scent of the leather as I heft a saddle onto Sandy's back deliver a comfort I've missed.

When I hear a vehicle approach, I glance out the wide barn door to spot Taylor's older RAV4 coming down the drive.

She gets out wearing a winter coat and mittens, and a knit hat with a ball on top pulled down over her head. I'm bundled up pretty good myself, knowing we plan to spend our time outside. Sun and forties or not, on the river it still feels like January in Kentucky.

Walking to meet her, I hear the front door and turn to see my mother step out on our big white-railed porch. "Hello and welcome, Taylor!" she calls. "It's so nice to see you other than just on quick stops into the bake shop. I was delighted when Luke told me he'd invited an old friend over."

My God, Mom. You're making this feel like high school. As in a little embarrassing.

She keeps going, though, with, "Make yourself at home. And I've heated up some hot chocolate for you both." It's only then that I notice her holding two steaming mugs. She's still pretty at sixty-two, with bouncy, shoulder-length silver hair and a few lines around the smile I haven't seen much of lately.

"That's so kind," Taylor says, switching her gaze from me to Mom, who now descends the wide front steps, cocoa in hand. "It's nice to see you, too, Mrs. Montgomery. And I'm so sorry for your loss."

Mom nods her thanks. "It's been hard, but I'm grateful I've got Luke here." Then she hands both mugs off to Taylor. "You two have fun and just let me know if you need anything."

Sheesh. It feels more like she's dropping us off at the movies or leaving us to play video games in the basement than sending us on a farm tour. "Sorry about that," I say softly after Mom's back inside.

As I take one of the mugs, our hands brushing through my gloves and her mittens, Taylor head shakes it away, adding, "She's very sweet."

"And apparently happy I have a friend," I add on a laugh. "But I shouldn't complain. This is the most cheerful I've seen her since Dad died."

"Then it's a good sign," Taylor says hopefully. "Back when *my* dad died, my mom really struggled. She tried to keep a brave face for me, but I know it challenged her."

"Your father was so young, too," I say. At thirteen, I couldn't conceive the true gravity of losing a parent. It makes me feel all the worse remembering how mean kids were when she was already dealing with so much. "You were really strong back then."

She only shrugs, though. "I didn't *feel* strong—but sometimes life is about rising to the occasion." Then she scrunches up her nose a little. "Guess I learned that young—for better or worse. Sometimes you just do what you have to."

"Glad you dressed warm," I tell her. She looks cute as hell in winter wear, her hair falling in ringlets around her face beneath her hat.

"You're wearing a cowboy hat," she points out as if I don't know, sounding amused. I suppose, even in Kentucky horse country, you don't see a lot of those if you're not directly on a horse farm.

"Keeps the sun out of my eyes and the rain off my neck," I inform her with a smile.

She tilts her head and somehow looks a little surprised as she adds, "It suits you."

We're walking as we talk, and I notice her studying the house. "It's so beautiful," she says. "I love all the gingerbread details. How old is it—do you know?"

I take a careful sip from my mug before answering. "If I'm remembering correctly, it was built in 1910." Then I point to the much smaller structure behind it, the one I exited just a little while ago. The same blue as the house, it's identically trimmed in small white spindles and lengths of intricately-carved wood. "This used to be a carriage house, but Dad had it converted into a guesthouse when I was a kid. He mostly used it as an office, but it's always come in handy on holidays when everyone's home. I'm staying there now just to give Mom some space."

"It's perfect," she replies, and as we turn the house's back corner, she gasps. "Oh, wow—there's even a gazebo?"

"Yeah," I tell her. "It's been there my whole life." And as we walk toward it, I find myself seeing the place through her eyes, almost as if for the first time. Funny the things you can miss even when they're right in front of you.

Stepping up into the big white gazebo, we sit side-by-side on a built-in bench facing the mighty Ohio, and Taylor lets out a dreamy sigh as she takes in the view. Across the mile-wide river, bare trees line the bank, and an eerie layer of mist hovers over the water's cold surface. "So you got to see this your whole life, every day, growing up? That must have been amazing."

"Guess I took it for granted," I confess. "You're right, though. It's pretty awesome."

"Peaceful," she observes. Then she looks over at me. "When *I* want to see the river, I have to go to Riverview Park behind Main Street. It's pretty dumpy, though." The observation comes with another cute scrunch of her nose and a bit of soft laughter. "Similar view, but this feels different. Almost... soothing. Like the kind of place where you can get away from everything but your own thoughts."

She says it like maybe she longs for that sometimes. But maybe we all do. "You could come here anytime you want," I tell her. "Mom wouldn't mind."

Though she gives her head a quick shake. "That's very kind, but I would never invade someone's privacy that way."

"Well," I say, half joking, half serious, "now I feel kind of guilty, having it all to ourselves while everyone else is going to the dumpy park in town." Because I'm suddenly seeing that it *is* soothing. Kind of like the horses. I never realized I had so much tranquility right here on the farm. Maybe I've just never thought about needing that before, even though my escape into nature out west surely means I did. It's strange to realize that all this time, all these years, there's been so much beauty right under my nose.

"Were there always horses here?"

I shift my gaze from the river to find Taylor glancing toward Scout and Duchess, two ponies meandering along just inside the white wooden fencing beyond the guesthouse.

"No, it was just empty fields until Mom and Dad bought the place, back before I was born. We've heard the area was prone to flooding back in the days before locks and dams, so I guess no one wanted to risk putting anything else here but the house and the inn. Both sit up a little higher than everything around them, and that's probably why—old flood concerns.

"Anyway," I go on, "my Grandpa Montgomery was the president of a bank in Louisville, and that got him prime grandstand seats at Churchill Downs for the Kentucky Derby. My dad's family went every year as he was growing up, and he fell in love with horses and horse racing. He started taking our family, too, when my brothers and I were just little kids."

"That sounds fun," she says in a way that reminds me she's probably never been to the derby, despite it happening only an hour away every May.

"I have mixed feelings about racing," I tell her, "but I loved getting to see the horses. By the time I was three or four, Dad had gotten the barn and fences built and bought a horse for every member of the family—a pony for me."

Her dreamy expression forces me to realize how fortunate I've been—without always taking the time to notice.

"That sounds incredible," she says. "Like a picture-perfect childhood."

"I guess it was," I have to admit. Sure, I spend a lot of time internally grousing about my dad, but in most ways, I had it really good.

When my phone buzzes in my pocket, I pull it out. "Sorry," I say. "Need to check. Just in case it's work."

"No problem."

But I must have made a face at the screen because she adds, "Or is there one? A problem?"

I shove the phone back away, not wanting to tell her. But I also don't want to lie, even about something small. "It's Jasmine."

She tries to hide it, but her expression changes just enough that I almost wish I'd lied. "Oh," she says in an effort to sound casual, like it's nothing. "So you still see her?"

"No," I answer quickly. "I haven't talked to her in years until she came to the funeral and..." I give my head a short, perturbed shake. "She keeps reaching out, and I'm not interested, but I'm also trying not to be cruel."

"You were always nice to everyone," she says as if trying to absolve me—perhaps then *and* now—from associating with Sweetwater's highest ranking "mean girl."

And for some reason, I need Taylor to know, so I blurt out unplanned, "I never really loved her. I tried to. I even thought I did for a while, but I didn't."

She simply looks at me, clearly speechless. Because I've created an awkward moment. When I just want to be open with her. Because even all these years later, I know she's one of the best people I've ever met. And there are just things I want her to understand. So I go for it. "Can I be real with you, Taylor?" I lean closer to ask.

"Of course," she answers softly.

Okay, here goes. "The truth is, I'm not sure I would have kept dating Jasmine so long except..." I stop, take a breath. Turns out this is actually kinda hard to say. "When my parents met her, my father really liked her. She was planning on med school back then, believe it or not, and my dad, of course, *loved* that. And what can I say?" I let out a small sigh. "I liked pleasing him. So little about me did."

When I gather the courage to raise my gaze to hers, she seems confused. "What do you mean, so little did? You were the star athlete. The most popular guy in school."

Oh, she doesn't know? It was never a secret among my friends, but my connection with Taylor was different, more isolated, so...maybe I never actually told her personal stuff? "Things weren't great between me and my dad," I inform her.

She blinks her surprise. "Really? Why?"

I don't talk much about this—it's just a thing in my life that's always been this way—but I try to explain. "He...valued academic achievement, not sports or other things I was good at." I offer up a shrug. "Maybe that seems odd, him being a horse guy—but horses were the only outdoor interest he ever had. He never even came to my games or track meets when I was growing up—it was only Mom. And after I got older, he never seemed particularly proud of my achievements."

"Maybe that was just his personality," she suggests. It's probably hard for her to conceive of a parent being any less than loving and supportive. "Was he the same way with your older brothers?"

But I guess I have to disabuse her of that notion. "No. Tom and Aaron were both a lot more like *him*. He was so damn proud of them for practicing law. And a lot *less* proud of his kid who quit school to go ride horses. Horses were a *pastime*, he informed me once on the phone. Not a job."

"That's a shame," she says, her voice brimming with compassion.

Yet I blow out a regretful sigh—because maybe I've been *too* real. "I probably sound like a whiny rich kid. But...when he actually *liked* the girl I was dating, it mattered. It shouldn't have, but it did."

"No," she's quick to interject. "That's not what I was thinking at all. I'm just surprised. I guess I heard you grumble about your dad now and then, but I had no idea what a big deal it was. I'm sorry you didn't have a better relationship with him."

"*I'm* sorry," I tell her, "that I hadn't outgrown caring about it by then. It would have saved me a lot of Jasmine-related headaches."

When she makes a slight face, I want to kick myself for bringing up her old nemesis yet again. I'm trying to reassure her Jasmine is out of my life for good, but I'm not sure I'm succeeding.

"So," Taylor says, letting her green eyes go wide, "Jasmine went to med school? Really? What happened?"

I shrug. "She didn't get in. Totally underestimated what it would take. So she decided to become a professional influencer instead. And the most surprising thing about *that* decision is that it actually worked. For a while, anyway."

"So the story going around about her talent agency boss is

true?" She sounds a little uncomfortable asking, like maybe it's wrong to gossip.

And maybe it is. But choices have consequences, and maybe being the topic of some hometown gossip is one of them for Jasmine. I keep it simple, though. "From what I hear. And it wouldn't shock me." Enough said.

Taylor must feel the same way, since she changes the subject. "Tell me more about Utah."

Works for me. "What do you want to know?"

I like watching her think. Or maybe I just like watching *her*. With a cute tilt of her head, she asks, "What was your job like on the ranch?"

Thinking back brings me a smile. "I loved it. Leading trail rides, taking care of the horses—those were good days. Easy days," I add reminiscently. "For the first time, I felt like I didn't have a care in the world. I did, of course. I had responsibilities. They were just ones I found fulfilling. And there was no dad pressuring me toward law school, or making me feel like a big disappointment because I wasn't chomping at the bit to live the life he wanted me to."

When she smiles back at me, I feel it to my core. "And then you started working for the outfitter place? How was that?"

I nod, remembering. "Also pretty great. Some days I worked in the shop, renting out equipment, but like I told you before, mostly I led hikes. My favorite was the Narrows in Zion. You hike up the Virgin River, *in* the river, on the rocks that line the shallow riverbed. You start out only up to your ankles—but keep going and you're eventually in pretty deep, which is when a guide becomes a good idea."

Her eyes have widened prettily. "That sounds intense."

"It can be. And it's cold without the right gear, but that's what outfitters are for." I end on a wink.

"And after that, you bought the place, right? So what are your workdays like now? Still leading hikes? Or doing other stuff?"

A sigh leaves me, the questions delivering a sense of letdown I didn't see coming. "Other stuff," I tell her. "Now I mainly run the business."

"And so you're happy out there?"

"It's an awesomely beautiful region. And I'm proud of my company."

This time when she tilts her head, she looks more inquisitive, like maybe she thinks she's caught me at something. "Is that your final answer?"

I let out a laugh. "Guess it wasn't much of one, huh?" I twist up my mouth a little, thinking it through. "Maybe I miss the outdoor work. The hikes. The horses." I glance over at Scout and Duchess, still near the fence, and tell her, "It's been nice hanging with these guys. Most of the eight we have here now are older horses who needed a retirement place. Mom and Dad never really planned to get back into the horse life when they moved home to Sweetwater, but they kept meeting people who needed to rehome their horses. And they had the space and means, so they started taking them in."

"That's so nice," she says.

"Yeah, I was glad when they did it. A few of them aren't rideable anymore or never were, but we don't care." Glancing down to see both of our mugs now empty, I suggest,

"Speaking of which, want to take a ride? I've got two saddled up and waiting for us in the barn."

Her eyes bolt open to leave her looking completely caught off guard. "Really? Because...I've never...I wouldn't know how."

But I just smile. "Don't worry—I'll teach you."

Taylor

I rest high atop a light brown mare with a black mane named Sugar—presumably because she's the color of brown sugar—while Luke sits next to me on a white horse called Sandy. I'm nervous, but doing okay—Sugar is patient and gentle, making this easier than I expected.

Before mounting his own ride, Luke reached up to cover my hand with his, showing me how to use the reins to guide her—and even our gloves didn't prevent me from feeling the warmth of his touch. Now he says, "When you're ready, give her a light tap with your heels to start her walking. Watch me."

He demonstrates, and I follow his example with my shoes tucked into the stirrups hanging down from the saddle. When Sugar ambles forward, a small gasp escapes me and I grip the saddle horn with my free hand to feel more secure.

"Look at you," Luke says, smiling over. "Riding a horse."

"Word of the day," I say. "Equestrian."

He lets out a soft, deep laugh.

"It's...kind of fun," I admit with a small grin, getting acclimated.

"Fun *and* practical," he teases. "I can show you more of the farm this way."

As we take a leisurely ride through the pasture, he points out other horses enjoying the sunny day. "That handsome guy is Star," he says of a sleek black horse with a white star on his forehead. "And that's Buttons. Who hates us, by the way, for giving him such a cutesy name—but my mother insisted. He came to us a few Christmases ago, and Dad and I agreed you don't name a mustang Buttons, but we lost that fight." He finishes on another laugh as I take in the rather wild-looking spotted horse who I concur is probably offended by his name.

"And up there by the road, under the trees," Luke goes on, pointing to a pretty palomino, "is Lady Jane. She's a Quarter horse. Used to be in shows."

"She looks like a dainty little lady," I observe.

"Yep, she's definitely the prissiest and most elegant resident in the barn," he confirms. Then he motions to the big white horse beneath him. "Sandy here became my dad's riding buddy. Dad was very fond of this guy and I think Sandy's wondering where he is. I've been trying to keep him company when I have the time, and hopefully I'll get him out for a few more rides while I'm here."

Walking Sugar alongside Sandy, I glance over at my companion and suggest, "It sounds like the horses were something you and your dad connected over."

Luke tosses me a thoughtful sideways glance from beneath the wide brim of his hat. That's something I like about grown-up Luke—he's not always quick to answer or to act like he knows everything; he takes things in and weighs them before responding.

"I never thought about it like that," he finally replies. "But maybe you're right. We didn't have *much* in common, but we did both love horses and care about their welfare. The older Dad got, in fact, the softer he became about them. He wasn't soft about much, but he cooed over horses the way most people do kittens or puppies."

As Sugar meanders through the field, I find the rhythm of her gentle gait relaxing, and a few moments of silence between Luke and I let me ponder everything around us. "It seems to me," I finally say, "that a lot of life is about meeting in the middle. I don't mean compromise exactly, but just figuring out where the middle ground lies. Like you and your dad clashing on some things, but still connecting through others. That's what we need for the town, a solution that brings business to Sweetwater without destroying our riverfront and your family home."

When he casts me a good-natured grin, I realize I've just stated the obvious. "It's not that I don't appreciate your optimism, Taylor, but I think if it was that easy, someone would have come up with this magical solution already, without a drywall factory entering into the mix."

"I know, I know," I agree. "It's just...now that I'm here, on your farm, it hurts my heart to think of this place being destroyed." I glance over at him on Sandy. "And where would the horses go?"

At this, his brow furrows. "Damn. That's a great—by which I mean troubling—question. Given that we've taken them all in from people who couldn't keep them, and that it's hard to find someone to do that."

I let out a long, despairing sigh. This conundrum was

already awful, but now it's also about the fate of the horses. "Then we have to find an answer that suits everyone," I insist. "I know I sound like a Pollyanna of the highest order, but surely there's some answer no one has thought of."

Just then, at the sound of a vehicle, we both glance back to see a shiny pickup rolling down the lane leading to the house and barn in the distance. "That's our farrier," Luke says, having explained earlier that one of the horses needs a new shoe. "Be okay without me for a few minutes?"

I peek down at Sugar, who I already feel an affinity for. "Will we be okay, Sugar?" I lean toward her head to ask, pleased when she actually turns to look at me.

Luke appears amused. "What did she say?"

I give him my bravest smile. "That we're good and you should go take care of her buddy, Ash."

As he kicks Sandy into a gallop and they go racing across the field back toward the barn, I grow a little nervous again, but I also feel accomplished. Maybe I've experienced this before, anytime I've attempted something new. Running a bake shop, for instance. Or starting community college, by myself for the first time since meeting Caroline, and realizing that being on my own for it was okay.

It's good to get out of your comfort zone from time to time. Life in the Sweetwater school system made that a terrifying proposition for a long while, but a lot has changed since then. A lot *inside me* has changed.

On some days, anyway. On others, old insecurities creep back in. Like the day I hid from Luke in the alleyway. I cringe remembering it.

Today, though, I feel almost like I *belong* in this lovely, bucolic world of his. Some people might dream of fairytale castles or lavish mansions, but for me, this farm has always been that not-quite-reachable place that looked like the perfect life.

Glancing around at the docile horses dotting the meadow, the white fencing, the clumps of trees and the gentle river flowing past, and then peeking back at the big, beautiful Victorian home, I marvel. It's a world Luke has chosen to leave—and yet he seems to love it here.

And I love being here *with* him. I love sharing this ride with him. I love hearing him tell me about the horses and his family and his life. I love looking over into those eyes made bluer by the winter sun overhead. I even love him in a cowboy hat, which I didn't expect. But he's turned into a more rugged, earthy man than I could have predicted in our youth, and I wasn't lying when I said it suited him.

It this...romance?

Or is it an old friend showing me his childhood home because it might soon be demolished?

I still don't know.

Yes, a lot has changed since high school, but it's still hard to believe Luke Montgomery could want me in any real way. After all, I'm not the queen bee; I'm not the head cheerleader or pageant princess. I'm the awkward girl with flour in her still-uncontrollable red hair.

And no matter how he tries to explain it away, it would seem Jasmine remains a factor in his life. As if I'm not confused enough by this situation, I also have to wonder how *she* figures in.

Do I hate that all these years later I'm still letting this girl get under my skin? Absolutely. But she's like a persistent mosquito that just keeps coming back.

When Luke returns a little while later, he shows me to the edge of the property about a mile down the river from the barn. As we both sit there on horseback, peering out over the peaceful Ohio, I suffer the urge to speak the truth now burning in my heart: *If all this was mine, I'd never let it go, and I'd never leave.*

But I hold my tongue. It sounds like the naïve proclamation of a poor girl getting her first taste of something grand. In fact, that's exactly what it is. I don't want to remind him how different we still are. And I don't want to pressure him when he's got enough pressures already.

Darkness falls early in wintertime, so as the sun dips to the west across the river, casting a ribbon of golden light across the water, he says, "We should head back."

When we reach the big barn, painted blue to match the other structures, Luke dismounts, then comes over to help me, gripping Sugar's bridle with one hand. "It's a big step down," he reminds me, and as I lift my right leg over the horse's back and lower it to the ground, his free hand is behind me, at my waist, steadying me. I lean slightly, instinctively, into the touch.

Together, we lead the horses into the barn and Luke shows me how to remove Sugar's saddle as he takes off Sandy's as well. Then he grabs brushes from a pegboard on the barn wall and instructs me in how to brush Sugar down after her ride.

"Last thing we do to end a ride around here," he tells me with a small smile, "is..." He reaches both hands into the pockets of his coat and pulls out an apple in each. "A treat. Kind of a thank you."

Handing me one, he says, "You want to put it in your palm, stretch your hand out flat, then hold it under her mouth and let her take it, careful to keep your fingers out of the way. Watch."

He demonstrates with Sandy, and I gape as the horse gobbles the entire apple down in one bite.

"They just eat the whole thing, core and all?"

He grins at my horse naïveté. "Core and all. Now you try."

I do as Luke did, careful about my fingers as I offer the apple to Sugar. She grabs it from my palm before I'm fully prepared, but it's okay—and leaves me with the impression that she and I are even better friends now. "Thank you for the ride," I tell her softly.

"Want to help me let Ash out?" Luke asks.

"What does that involve?"

"Um, mostly just watching me let Ash out," he answers with a grin.

The sun sinks fast toward the horizon now, the day turning quickly dusky and colder as I follow him toward a stall housing a big gray stallion.

"Most nights, we stable them all," he explains. "Everyone has their own philosophies on that, but we like being able to check on them daily to make sure they're all healthy. Occasionally, though, we let them pasture overnight, and we'll do that tonight, just to let Ash roam after a day of being cooped up. They can all get back into the barn if they want to."

He enters Ash's stall, then unlatches a door there, sliding

it open. He doesn't have to prod the big horse—Ash turns and trots out on his own. Then Luke goes about opening *all* the stable doors, sending Sandy and Sugar back out into the field as well.

When Luke announces it's dinnertime for the gang, I walk with him as he loads grain into a long trough outside the barn. The three horses nearby head straight to it, and the rest can be seen coming from different parts of the farm after Luke rings the big, traditional dinner bell mounted on a thick post outside the barn.

"They don't fight over the food?" I ask.

Luke shakes his head. "Nah—they have hay in their stalls and some in the pasture to eat whenever they want, so official mealtimes are pretty peaceful."

A few minutes later, he walks me to my car, and I'm sad the day is ending.

"I had a great afternoon," he tells me. "Thank you for coming."

"It's beautiful here, and I loved learning about the horses, and riding Sugar. Thank you for asking me."

And then there we stand, beside my car door. And I'm glad it's mostly dark now because I fear my face is red. Not from the cold, but from the fact that I'm suddenly wondering if he's about to kiss me. Because that's how it seems. Like this *is* romance, and not just a farm tour.

It's one of those moments when only a few seconds feels like an eternity. I wait awkwardly, uneasily. I've certainly been kissed before, but never by Luke Montgomery. I can't quite meet his gaze, so I've lowered my eyes. I'm seventeen all over again.

Finally, his gloved hand cups one side of my face and he bends...to lower a sweet kiss to my cheek. "Goodnight, Taylor," he says, voice soft and low.

"Goodnight, Luke." It comes out in a whisper, unintended.

And then I'm in my car, buckling up, starting the engine, making my way back down the now-dark lane, headlights illuminating the path—but it's all happening on autopilot. Because how is it possible that of all the kisses I've ever received, this is the one—a mere cheek kiss!—I feel the most? It ripples from head to toe, still. My skin tingles all the way home.

11

JANUARY 17

Luke

The last place I would have expected to find myself a few weeks ago was sitting around a makeshift fire pit in Sweetwater, Kentucky, tossing back a couple of cold ones with my old buddies, TJ Browerton and Billy Finch. In the back lot of Billy's garage on the edge of town, no less, surrounded by stacks of old tires and a collection of vehicles in need of repair. What it lacks in ambience, though, it makes up for in other ways. It's good to be with my old friends.

"This almost reminds me," I say, "of summer nights on the ranch outside Springdale when I first moved out west."

"Except this is a far cry from summer," TJ points out, zipping up his parka.

Yep, without the fire and the alcohol, we'd be freezing. "Guess I meant the vibe. Friends, no pressures, all that."

Across the crackling flames from me, Billy gives his head an inquisitive tilt beneath a worn ball cap bearing the name of his business. "So what the hell led you to Utah anyway, bruh?"

I can only laugh. It's the question of the month. "Guess I just fell in love with the great outdoors," I reply. "Maybe I always was, but it never hit me so hard until I ended up on the ranch. I just...didn't want to come back inside."

Looking back on it, it feels like a long time ago. "And I get why my parents were outraged. Probably seemed like I was going nowhere fast. But I was tired of them pushing me toward law school. And in the end, things worked out for the best."

That's when I notice TJ, my one-time best friend who I lost touch with around that time, eyeing me peculiarly.

"What?" I ask.

"Okay, get ready for it," he tells me. "I'm a little drunk, so I'm gonna speak from the heart."

"Uh oh," I say.

Billy laughs, but Teej only smiles.

Then he goes quiet and I have to prod him. "What? Out with it."

"Look...I know you have a good life out there, and you've built a successful business. But the truth is, I've missed having you around, man."

No one laughs at that. In fact, the declaration casts a somber pall over the gathering. TJ and I were college roommates for three years and I kinda left him high and dry in that regard. Finally, I say, "Same. But sometimes life leads in unexpected directions."

"I, for one, admire the hell outta you," Billy tells me. "Starting a whole new life somewhere far away takes guts."

I just shrug. "Believe it or not, it seemed like the easiest thing in the world. It felt like escape. And freedom. From my father."

"Listen," TJ says then, "I know you and your dad were never close, but...how are you handling this? Gotta be tough losing a parent. Especially with no warning."

As usual when people give me their condolences, though, I just shake it off. "I'm mainly worried about Mom," I tell them. "Otherwise, I'm fine."

At this, my old teammates exchange glances, and TJ slants me a pointed look. "Dude, really? Your dad died and you're fine? You can be real with us, ya know."

Yet I only shrug. "Like you said, we weren't close."

"But...your face right now..." Billy's eyes narrow on me in suspicion.

And I feel my eyebrows shoot up. "What *about* my face?"

Both hesitate, until Billy waves it away with, "Nothing, bruh. Forget I brought it up."

Damn, what the hell is happening with my face? And why does my chest feel so tight? I answer my own questions by tossing back another swig of beer, trying to wash them away.

"I think this conversation has gotten too serious," TJ declares.

I say, "I couldn't agree more. Let's lighten it up, huh?"

And Billy locks his gaze on me to ask, "You ever think about coming home? For good?"

I just flash him an accusing look. "Yep, nothing serious about that."

"I'm just saying...now that your dad's gone, don't you worry about your mom? That she's gonna be lonely in that big old house with none of her kids nearby?"

"Shit," I mutter on a sigh. The fact is... "I haven't had time to think that far ahead." And I don't like the thought. "But at least Aaron's only a couple hours away in Cincy. Still a lot of big questions to be answered—about everything—but I couldn't move back here if I wanted to. I've got a thriving business out west."

They both nod in understanding as TJ replies, "Well, I'm sure it'll all work out."

The three of us fall silent then, nursing our beers and soaking in the night. It's nice catching up, but this conversation has become less the distraction I'd hoped for and more about my current concerns. Between all the responsibilities falling to me right now—plus this new added worry about Mom—who can think very far into the future? The *right now* is keeping me stressed enough on its own.

"Speaking of Utah, you guys should come out," I suggest, still trying to lighten the mood. "Hike the Mighty Five with me." I know the big five Utah parks like the back of my hand because it's my business to. "We'd have a great time."

"That sounds good," Billy answers, more upbeat.

And TJ adds, "Yeah, I'd be into that. Maybe this summer after school lets out."

Billy points to the cooler at his side, asking me with his

eyes if I want another, but I say, "Nah," giving my head a short shake, thinking I'll be heading home soon. He gets one out for himself and pops the top.

And that's when TJ asks, "Any idea what you're gonna do about this drywall plant situation?"

I tilt him an annoyed look. "I see we're still sticking to lighthearted subjects."

A small, guilty chortle leaves him. "I know, I know—but it's on everyone's mind now, night and day."

"Mine included," I inform him. "I feel like I'm carrying the weight of the world, or at least Sweetwater, on my shoulders."

"Sorry," he says, contrite. "I guess you *do* have a lot to deal with. So much for relaxing with your old buddies and an adult beverage, huh?"

But I head shake it away. "No worries. Like you said, it's there all the time, even when I'm trying to shut it off." Then I look to Billy. "*You* own a business in this town. What do *you* want to happen? You said no to the factory at the meeting, but has anything changed for you since then?"

Billy takes a swallow from his newly-opened can, then says, "Tell you the truth, I'm not sure. Do I think bringing more people to this town would help it? Of course. But do I think some giant factory on the river would ruin the place?" He lets out a sigh. "Of course."

I nod, remembering Taylor's pie-in-the-sky idea of some magical, outside-the-box solution coming along. I only wish it were that simple. "The more I think about it," I tell my friends, "the more confused I become."

12

JANUARY 19

Luke

Mom and I sit down to lunch in front of the big picture window overlooking the river, trying to hash out the future. We've got less than two weeks to decide Sweetwater's fate.

"As I've told you," she says, "I'll be fine with whatever's decided. Yes, I love our home, but I'm also open to a new start. And to tell you the truth, the house feels...a little too big to me without your father here. Maybe I need a smaller place."

Neither of us have yet touched the grilled chicken salad she put together for us—I guess we've got other things on our minds besides eating. I blow out a sigh and pose the question that's been weighing on me for a couple of days now. "Are you gonna be all right? Living on your own with all of us far away?"

She's a young sixty-two, but I'm not sure what her life will be about now. For a long time, it was about caring for this big house and her family. After her sons left, it became about spending time with Dad. They've traveled a lot in the last ten years, and they took day trips on weekends to wineries or historic restaurants she searched out online. She likes to read and watch historical documentaries, but will that be enough? She used to have friends, but they've all moved away over time as Sweetwater fell deeper into decline.

I can see in her eyes now that maybe she's starting to wonder the same thing. "To be honest, Luke, I'm not entirely sure." Then she musters up a brave smile. "I may need to find some hobbies or do some volunteer work. This house has always kept me busy, even when we didn't live in it and I was driving down to check on it. And I've enjoyed caring for it— but as I say, the appeal of that might be over." She shakes her head then, looking forlorn. "On the other hand, it's a beautiful life here, so I'm sure I can adjust to it alone. Or, again, adjust to something new, too." She meets my gaze, tilting her head. "I suppose there's a part of me that can't imagine staying in this house and a part of me that can't imagine leaving." She laughs. "I'm not being much help on this, am I?"

"It's okay, Mom," I assure her. "You don't have to have all the answers right now. I just want to make sure you'll be okay."

"Well, I'm certain I will because I have you to help me."

Her expression holds an almost out-of-the-ordinary affection. She's always been a loving mom, but I fear she feels a little abandoned by her two older boys, and a little afraid of this new life she didn't expect.

"Of course you do," I promise her.

"I'm sorry all this got dropped on you. I know it wasn't in your plans."

It's the first time she's acknowledged that since the abrupt change of executor.

"None of this was in *anyone's* plans," I remind her. And then I recall something Taylor said the other day. I didn't realize then how much it might apply to where I am right now. "But sometimes you just have to rise to the occasion. So I'm rising to it, and so are you." I give Mom a smile.

She returns it. "I guess I am." The small smile fades just as quickly as it came, though. "Even if it's hard. Some mornings I wake up still surprised to realize I'm alone in bed, and the reality hits me all over again. I thought we'd have so many more years together."

"I know," I say, squeezing her hand. "I know."

I still have no idea if she'll find ways to be happy when I go back to Utah, but I definitely won't let her feel abandoned by anyone else, that's for sure. Starting to think about Mom's future adds a lot more questions to the mix, but the kind that'll only be answered as some time passes.

So for this moment, I turn back to the more immediate one—whether or not to sell the farm.

"One way of looking at the Northcutt deal," I say, moving on, "is that maybe progress is inevitable. It's the same old story, right? That progress can't be stopped? If we don't sell, who's to say they don't find property just a few miles down the road and it still ruins Sweetwater?"

Mom finally picks up her fork and takes a bite of her salad, and so do I. Maybe it's easier to discuss the fate of a whole town than how much she's misses my father. "You're right," she replies. "That could happen. I'm not sure I'd like living here if I glanced out the window to see a big factory right down the river. And then we'd have to worry about the horses, too."

I narrow my gaze on her. "What do you mean?"

"Once, on one of our winery trips, your father and I drove past a big drywall plant along the river not far from Cincinnati, and a horrible white dust covered *everything*. Every bush and tree and blade of grass. It was just awful. I Googled about it, and I learned the company was ordered to clean it up and do better, but the lesson is that you just never know what you're letting yourself in for when change comes."

This has my head about to explode—I didn't even know something like that could happen. But whether right here or somewhere up the road... "That sounds extremely sketchy, like it could cause serious health concerns."

"It would probably never happen here, but who can say?"

I again shift my gaze out the window to this view I've always had but, sadly, never appreciated. "And maybe I'm wrong—maybe if we turn them down, they'll be forced to go someplace else entirely. When Taylor was here, she fell in the love with the place. It reminded me that maybe we take it for granted, that maybe it's worth saving. Not just for the sake of Sweetwater, but for the sake of the farm itself. Not to mention the horses."

Across the table, Mom's eyes light up in a way I've rarely

seen since Dad's passing. "Taylor sounds like a smart young woman. Tell me about her and you."

I actually can't believe it's taken her this long to come at me with this. "We go back a long way," I answer, deciding to keep it simpler than it is. "I wanted to ask her out in high school, but it didn't work out."

"And now?"

"Now...I like her."

She looks unimpressed. "That's it? You like her?"

I just laugh. "What are you looking for here, Mom? I just met her again after fifteen years. And in case you haven't noticed, my plate's a little full right now, so I'm not thinking much beyond the next few days."

She lets out an acceptant sigh. "I guess that's fair. You've had a lot heaped on you all at once."

Has Taylor stayed on my mind since she came for that visit? Absolutely. Do I remember how much I wanted to kiss her but didn't, because she suddenly looked so shy, not even making eye contact with me? For sure.

It left me thinking maybe she just wasn't into it, that maybe all we were ever meant to be is friends. And that maybe the way I feel when I'm with her—like life is suddenly better, easier, happier—just means I'm not able to tell the difference between a girl who wants to be kissed and a girl who only wants to be my pal.

When we talked that night at the Little Dipper about the past, I thought maybe she'd be interested in something more —but I know how to take a hint. And besides, it's not like I have time for romance while I'm here anyway.

13

JANUARY 21

Taylor

As big, heavy snowflakes begin to fall outside the window of the Sweetheart Bake Shop, I stand inside, alone but for Maggie, who's curled up asleep in her pink bed. It's been a quiet business day, and I'm about to shut the doors early as I sometimes do in winter when things are slow and darkness is about to descend.

But first I reach for the valentine box. It's a habit. Yes, I'm on the lookout for rogue orders, but I actually *enjoy* rifling through it every day or two. To see and touch the memory that is the box itself, to run my fingers over the childhood valentines that line it, somehow feels safe and familiar, bringing back sweet recollections of my dad. But at the same time, the business cards my customers drop inside remind me that life goes on, and that it's always changing, and that good memories—and also bad—just slowly become the fabric of our lives.

Though maybe the notion of memories fading into the background felt truer before Luke and Jasmine suddenly turned back up in town, almost at the same time. The valentines in the box and the memories they conjured felt nostalgic, like old news. Now, they don't feel so old. Things that seemed long since over and done don't feel so finished anymore. I've been transported back to old times and old emotions more than once.

"But I'm not that girl anymore," I insist in a whisper to no one.

No, I'm the girl who couldn't hold eye contact with Luke Montgomery the other night when he was about to kiss me. I roll my eyes at my own behavior.

Running my fingertips across the aging cards that line the box's lid, I'm remembering the little slip of paper that once got stuck there—when the front door opens and two women step inside from the cold. "Welcome in," I say, promptly sliding the lid back on.

Bundled up in coats and gloves, they both appear awestruck as they look around.

"It's as cute as it seemed online," one of them declares from beneath a red knit hat. "Hearts everywhere!"

"And oh my gosh, look at the display case," the other gushes, pushing a fur-rimmed hood off her head to reveal long, ebony locks underneath. "All the heart-shaped cookies and cupcakes! And that heart cake is so cute!" It's a lemon cake with icing drizzled in a criss-cross pattern, finished with colored confetti candies sprinkled on top. "And the scents in here." She stops to breathe it all in. "It's like heaven. If heaven is filled with cake. And surely it must be!"

We all share a small laugh over that, and I reply, "Thank you so much," pleased. "Glad you like the place."

"What gave you the idea?" The lady with the hood asks. "To make everything heart-shaped."

"Well, the place was once called the Sweetheart Diner," I explain. "And my dad also inspired me—he noticed hearts everywhere and even made this box for me when I was a little girl." As I hold it up to show them, they ooh and ahh their admiration.

"He must be very proud," says the one in the hat.

Deciding to spare them the he-died-when-I-was-twelve story, I just say, "He is." Since I know that's true anyway, whether or not he's here to tell me, and whether or not the shop lasts for decades more or ultimately dies a premature death if the whole town finally goes belly up.

When I ask what brings them in, the hood-wearer tells me they're road-tripping from Tennessee to Indiana to see a friend and decided to look for some local color on the way. "We found your shop online and had to come. We want to pick up some yummies for our visit while we're here!"

Ah, if only more people took the slow roads and looked for the local color. Then again, Sweetwater has even almost run out of *that*, now that I think about it. But not completely. "If you haven't eaten yet and want a good burger or some soft-serve ice cream, check out the Little Dipper about a mile south of here on the left."

"Oh, I think we passed that on our way into town," the hat says. "But maybe we'll go back."

"That reminds me," the hood chimes in, "we passed a pretty farm near there—horses up by the fence, and a gorgeous blue house. We were wondering if that's a place where you can ride horses, or even just pet or feed them. We were thinking our kids would love something like that if we made a return trip with them in better weather."

"But I said it looked privately owned," the hat adds.

"Oh, I know the place," I assure them. "And yeah, it's just a family farm where they take in horses who need homes."

The hat presses her hand to her chest. "Oh my God, that's so sweet."

I can't help but agree. "I know, right?"

"Well," the hood says, "they should...I don't know—let people pay a small fee to pet the horses. Just to go toward their expenses."

I keep to myself that the Montgomery family doesn't need the money, and instead tell them, "We don't get many out-of-towners, unfortunately. You know how it is—most people take the interstate and only get off for gas or fast food. Seventy-one passes right by, but our nearest exit is miles away."

The hood raises her eyebrows in speculation. "Who knows. Give people some reasons to stop and maybe they would. I mean, heart-shaped baked goods were enough for us. Horses might be enough for someone else."

The friendly ladies order up two dozen cookies and the drizzled lemon cake, and while I'm packing up the order, they drop business cards in the valentine box and coo over

Maggie with, "This is the cutest little dog," and, "Look, her collar even has hearts on it!" And the whole time I'm thinking: Ah—wouldn't it be great if a few horses were enough to revive the town? But I know it'll take more than that to bring Sweetwater back to life.

As I'm saying goodbye a few minutes later, hoping they pass back through, I find myself wondering what could make a few horses into more than—well, just a few horses. And as the door closes behind them, I notice a big fat snowflake has blown in to land on my welcome mat. It melts quickly, but not before I notice it's shaped like a heart.

14

JANUARY 22

Luke

Two fresh inches of snow last night has given way to sunny skies today. I've spent the morning tending the horses, and now I'm hanging out in the gazebo, taking in the view. Only nine days left until the Northcutt deadline. And it doesn't matter how many people I ask or how many lists of pros and cons I make—no good answer reveals itself.

As my chest tightens, I'm tempted to saddle up Sandy for a ride, but that seems irresponsible when there are a million estate issues to deal with. I'm about to head back to the guest-house office when my phone buzzes and I glance down to see a text—from Taylor.

Not gonna lie—my heartbeat kicks up as I swipe to see what she's sent.

Hope you're home. Headed your way. Sorry no notice, but I have an idea that could help the whole town. Maybe you'll think it's crazy, but maybe you won't. Word of the day: Solution! (Maybe.)

I blink and read it again. I can't imagine what she has to say. I just keep staring at my screen, almost wondering if I'm dreaming.

But stop. Rein in your expectations. Because maybe it will be a crazy idea, or at least something that won't work. So don't get excited.

That's tricky, though, with my heart beating like a drum in my chest. I'm not even sure if it's about this idea of hers or just getting to see her when I least expected it.

That's not my normal reaction to a woman—I'm generally cooler. But everything with Taylor seems different. She's not my regular type. I don't usually get rejected by girls I pursue, but with her, I do—whether or not it's intentional. I don't typically have to wonder how a woman feels about me, but with her, I just can't tell.

When I hear her car coming up the drive, I realize I haven't texted her back.

In the gazebo, I type. *Second word of the day: Intrigued.*

I hit Send and, a moment later, turn my head to see her walking around the house in fur-trimmed snow boots and the same cute hat from our last visit. My palms begin to sweat in my gloves and it hits me: *Damn, I like her so much. Too much.*

"Hi," she says, stepping into the shade of the gazebo.

"Hey."

She flashes a pretty smile. "The house and farm look beautiful covered in snow."

I glance around at the roofs dripping with icicles, the boughs of pine trees dusted in white, and once again, she's making me take it all in through fresh eyes. "You're right," I agree, letting my eyebrows knit. "Though I'm starting to feel like I miss a lot."

"What do you mean?" She sits down beside me on the built-in bench.

"You just kinda make me see things differently, that's all."

"Well," she says, giving her head an optimistic tilt, "maybe I'm about to make you see *your whole farm* differently."

I lower my chin in hesitant anticipation. "Okay. Whatever it is, let 'er rip."

"Yesterday, two women came in the bake shop," she begins, and goes on to tell me about their interest in being able to stop and visit the horses.

And I'm pretty sure whatever she's about to suggest isn't gonna fly—until she adds, "I know, of course, that's not enough to make a business. But I fell asleep still thinking about it, and this morning, I woke up with more of an answer."

With the tension mounting now, I use my hand to rush her along. "And? The suspense is killing me."

"Okay, what about..." she begins, "a horse park and sanctuary? A horse park for more horses who need homes—and for other horses who are good for trail rides. People could ride horses, watch horses, pet horses, feed horses, learn about horses. There could be educational talks and demonstrations. There could be displays and concessions. You already have the core of what you need to build it right here. You'd only have to add to what the farm already is.

"And sure, there are plenty of places where you can pay for a horseback ride, but the park and sanctuary aspects would make this more unique. More of a destination. A Kentucky hotspot.

"Would it bring in the new population and money the drywall plant would? No. But would it draw new traffic to Sweetwater that might spill over into the rest of the town and, at the very least, stand to help the inn and the Little Dipper? Yes. And it certainly wouldn't hurt anyone by destroying the river view."

She's been talking rapidly this whole time and now finally stops to take a breath. "What do you think?"

It's a lot to take in. Transforming our family home into a public attraction. Starting a second business. And the reality of, indeed, turning down the money offered by Northcutt. Even though I haven't wanted to take it, my brothers will be livid.

Yet...it's a vision I can see in my mind immediately.

It would take some money—we'd need more horses, more stalls, and maybe even more land. I wonder if Hank would be willing to part with some of the inn's grounds—maybe the influx of funds would be a good tradeoff for him. It would also take hiring staff, buying additional equipment, and creating a parking lot, not to mention putting together a general business model: How much would we charge for what? For rides versus a petting zoo type experience? I wonder if there's any funding available for places that save horses from euthanasia.

That's my business brain kicking into gear, but my heart is telling me, "My dad would love this idea. My brothers might not, but...well, that can be worked around. And I'll have to do a lot of number-crunching and research and thinking through the logistics to figure out if it would be profitable, but personally, I think it's...brilliant."

As her pretty eyes widen, she actually looks surprised. "Really?"

I give her a smile. "Really."

She exhales a big breath I didn't realize she was holding. "Because I didn't know what you would think, or if there would instantly be some reason you'd hate it or know for sure it wouldn't work."

I shake my head, still smiling at the gorgeous redhead next to me. "Nope, I love it. And you're right—it wouldn't bring big money rolling into town on day one, but...I could see this being viable, a thing we could advertise, plan events around. Like you said, make it a destination." Then, still gazing into her gorgeous green eyes, I tell her exactly what I'm thinking. "I always knew you were smart. But why was I so dumb?"

She looks a little confused. "Dumb?"

And I decide not to hold back, to just go for it. "It was dumb of me in high school not to see how attracted I was to you until it was pretty much too late. And it was dumb to let one rejection drive me to the wrong girl when I should have just talked to you about it. I've always thought of you as the one who got away, and since getting back to town, seeing you again, I'm having some big regrets about that."

She appears caught off guard. Understandably. I just said some huge things without quite planning to. I sense her remembering what happened—or didn't happen—between us back then, until finally she says, "We were both kids, doing the best we could at the time. And for what it's worth, I wish I'd done things differently, too."

At this, my eyebrows shoot up. "You? What do you mean?"

She offers up an uncertain shrug. "Well, I obviously wasn't the most confident girl. I wish I'd been more resilient, tougher, braver. I wish I'd been the kind of person who would have just gone to the dance by myself to begin with."

I let out a sigh. "I guess it's easy to woulda, coulda, shoulda when it's all in the past. But being a teenager wasn't for the faint of heart."

We exchange small, understanding smiles—though that's when she scrunches up her nose to say, "Regardless, I guess we just weren't meant to be."

"Well, it doesn't have to stay that way," I assure her. And as I drop my gaze from her emerald eyes to her full lips, I know that, at last, I'm about to kiss her. "In fact, I'm starting to think we fit pretty damn well together."

Like before, she seems timid, her lashes lowered—but then she's bold enough to peek up at me. Like maybe she wants this connection as badly as I do. It's all the encouragement I need.

Placing my hand on her shoulder, I lean in, catch the

inviting scent of cake or something sweet hanging about her, and—

"Hello again, Taylor!"

I stop, flinch, and look up. My well-meaning mother has just come out the back door of the house, carrying two mugs.

"I have hot chocolate!"

I could kill her.

Taylor

Every cell of my body is on high alert. He was starting to kiss me—only now he can't.

"I didn't know we had company, but I happened to glance out the kitchen window and here you are. It's so nice to see you again."

Something inside me wilts like a hothouse flower suddenly put out in the cold as Mrs. Montgomery walks into the gazebo bearing mugs with horses painted on them.

"Thank you," I say, taking one. "That was so thoughtful."

"Well, it's sunny but still cold. Believe me, after all these years, I know the weather on this river well."

She goes on about snow and the forecast and other things I only half hear. Because even though I was ready for it, my heart on fire for him, maybe a part of me is almost relieved by the interruption.

Did I want to kiss him? Of course. But if a kiss on the cheek from him left me spinning inside, what will a real kiss do?

And...just where do I think romance with Luke Montgomery would lead anyway? I can't pretend any feelings I'd have for him would be casual—because they wouldn't. It's an impossibility. I mean, the very idea of his mouth on mine is turning me inside out. And no matter his regrets over our past misunderstanding, and no matter what happens with this farm, he doesn't even live here anymore.

I'm dying to be kissed by Luke—but do I want to end up back where I was in high school? Crazy about a guy who's leaving soon?

"Will you stay for lunch, Taylor?" I tune back in to the conversation to hear his mother ask.

I haven't even looked at Luke since his mom came out—because I can't. I might melt in the heat of his eyes given the seductive gaze he was casting before the kiss that wasn't. Which feels sort of like the *dance* that wasn't. A lot more *wasn'ts* with Luke, it seems, than things that actually happen, and I'm not sure it's anyone's fault—just the way things keep turning out.

"Thanks, but I can't. I need to get back to the shop," I claim. I totally *could*—Geneva and Kyra are both there right now—but I'm not going to. "I just came to tell Luke an idea I had—which I'm sure he'll share with you. So thank you so much for the hot chocolate, but I'll have to decline. Take care."

And with that, I shove the mug back into her hand and rush away without even a glance behind me.

Real smooth, Taylor. Real smooth.

I regret it before I even reach my car. But it's too late to go back.

And if a fear for my heart drove me to leave, maybe I should put the pedal to the metal and keep going.

Luke

"I'm so sorry Taylor had to rush off," Mom says after she's gone.

"Me, too." *You have no idea, Mom.*

Peering down at me, still holding the mugs, she asks, "I didn't interrupt anything, did I?"

When I raise my gaze to hers without even the hint of a smile, she gets the picture. "Oh. Oh no. I'm so sorry, honey."

Letting out a sigh, because my mother shouldn't have to apologize for being nice, I pat the spot on the bench Taylor just vacated. "Sit down, Mom. It's okay."

When she does, I finally accept one of the mugs—and find her grimacing in my direction. "If I messed something up, it's not okay at all." Then she leans closer and, despite our complete privacy, whispers, "Is romance brewing?"

I don't normally talk to my mother about my love life, but since she suddenly seems to be right in the middle of it, I confide in her, just a little. "I didn't really think so, but... maybe it is."

"Well, how wonderful! Tell me more."

I look at her, this woman who raised me, this woman who I've spent more time with in the last two weeks than in the last two years. Part of me doesn't really want to get into the nitty-gritty of my long past with Taylor Mulvaney, but...her eyes are so wide and she's focusing on me so intensely. Maybe she's trying to find things to care about right now, things that aren't the husband she just buried.

And so before I know it, words start coming out. I tell Mom the whole story of the lost invitation to the sweetheart dance, and how devastated I was when Taylor didn't show, and how tough that kind of thing has always been for me.

"It's a normal reaction," she responds. "No one likes feeling rejected."

Yet I argue. I mean, we're in this now, really dissecting it, so why not tell it like it is? "But me—I *overreact*. Every time. I've broken up with girls over minor slights. Even *before* the sweetheart dance, I took it too personally if somebody didn't show up where they were supposed to, or said the smallest thing that made me feel put down. I guess it always just reminded me of Dad," I conclude.

I instantly regret the last part, though.

"I'm sorry, Mom. I shouldn't have said that. I know he was a good husband and you loved him. I loved him, too. I just..."

"It's okay, Luke—you can tell me," she promises when I trail off. "You just what?"

I hesitate, but finally go on. Even if I soften it a little—for her benefit as much as my own. "I just never felt like I measured up in his eyes. And he...wasn't really there for me." I lift my gaze to hers. "Surely you saw it—you know he never came to my games. And he definitely didn't care about what mattered to me."

I'm a little surprised at my own honesty given that we've never talked about this before. It was always, "Your father's tired after a long day, but *I'll* be there cheering you on." And eventually it wasn't even that—it was just her showing up and him staying home, undiscussed. My friends have always known Dad and I had issues, but acknowledging it to *her* feels different, bigger.

She stays quiet for a moment—until she says, "It was wrong of him, not showing up for you in those ways. It was selfish—one of his worst traits." Taking my mug from me, she sets both of them down between us and closes my gloved hands in hers. "But I hope you know how much he loved you."

When I don't respond to that, though, she takes a deep breath, then looks me in the eye. "Okay, I'm about to tell you something that has to stay just between us."

I have no idea where this is going.

"And it's that you were always the best of my boys, with the best heart." She squeezes my hands. "I'm proud of Tom and Aaron—of course. But I'm the most proud of *you*. You had the most to overcome."

"I did?" I ask, a little dumbfounded.

She gives a solemn nod. "It's hard when you don't share the same passions or goals as your parents. It takes courage to go your own way in life. And you've done it so beautifully." Her expression grows bittersweet. "Yes, there were times we worried for your future—but you proved us so wrong. Your father told me so time and again."

This is the most shocking part yet, and I narrow my gaze on her doubtfully. "Seriously?"

She answers with a small smile. "I think it almost embarrassed him to be wrong because he was so accustomed to being right, being in control. But he would look up information about your business online and show me. He would say, 'Our Luke has done good,' or 'Guess he knew what he was doing all along.'"

I respond with only a skeptical look. Are we talking about the same guy here?

"He should have told you he was proud," she goes on, "but he was just never that kind of man. Same as his father before him. Somehow it was easier for him to tell *me*. And maybe he didn't know you needed to hear it. But I promise you, it was there."

Having stunned me into silence at this point, she keeps going.

"He was never a soft father, I'm aware. He was raised by a gruff man who believed there was only one path to success, and he became a similar man. To tell you the truth, it was good to see him a little humbled by your accomplishments—he once admitted to me with a little grin that maybe this meant he didn't know everything after all."

I swallow past the annoying lump that's risen in my throat as a cold breeze streams through the gazebo. I'm not even sure I'm buying all this—because maybe she's just deluding herself. Regardless, though, it's a lot to take in.

"But I'm sorry if he failed to make you feel his love," she tells me. "And he would be so, so proud of all you're doing for me, and for the family—when your brothers...aren't."

I've stayed quiet a long time, and I don't say anything to that, either—I'm angry at my siblings for hurting her with their neglect, yet acknowledging *that* isn't what she needs right now.

As for all she's just said, whether it's real—or just something she's conflated into being bigger than it was—I feel closer to *her* than I have since leaving home. So I finally pull her into a tight hug and whisper, "I know how hard it is on you losing him."

After a moment, she peeks up from our embrace. "Just remember that he loved you very much, Luke. He simply wasn't good at showing it."

Love is a hard thing to measure when it's not acknowledged, so as the hug comes to an end, I'm still digesting it all. "Okay," I promise quietly.

"Well," she says then, smoothing her coat and lifting a cocoa mug to sip from, "now that we have that settled, Taylor said there was something you wanted to tell me."

15

JANUARY 25

Taylor

Caroline waits at her usual table, wearing a stylish violet sweater and nibbling on a heart-shaped chocolate chip cookie. Geneva is making brownies in the kitchen, and I've just put some pies in the oven, so I decide to take a break, joining my friend with two pink coffee mugs.

"Beware, Satan," Caroline hisses softly, and I follow her eyes toward the window in time to catch sight of Jasmine walking past in her long runway model's stride. It's quick, but I glimpse pointy-heeled leather boots and a red blazer cut at fashion-forward angles. Her long blonde locks look to be in some elaborate updo today. As always, it's way too much for rundown little Sweetwater, but otherwise enviably stunning.

"Why on earth does she keep dressing for L.A. when she's in rural Kentucky?" Caroline asks more loudly.

"Maybe that's all she owns," I say. "Rodeo Drive clothes."

Caroline raises her eyebrows. "Have you seen her Instagram?"

I sit up a little straighter, intrigued. "No. You know I'm not into all that, and that Kyra does the social media for the shop." Honestly, those pictures I once saw of Jasmine with Luke online just soured me on that whole world.

"Well, I do my own for the deli," my bestie reminds me, "so I admit to having taken a peek." She begins playing with her phone as she goes on.

"So by 'taken a peek,'" I say accusingly, "you mean you've completely stalked her."

"Tomato, tomahto," she answers with a shrug. "Word on the street is that she's lost seventy-five percent of her followers since her fall from Hollywood grace. Now, mind you, that still leaves over a million. But they're dropping like flies and I think she's struggling to hold on to her brand."

Now Caroline turns the phone to me, and on the screen I see the online handle, *ItsJasmineDupree*. "She used to be AllThatJasmine," Caroline informs me, "but I think there are too many Jasmines using something similar now, so I guess she changed it."

I read the short bio out loud. "*Influencer, fashion icon, and connector to the stars. L.A. vibes. Hollywood is my playground.*" I can't hold in a judgmental laugh at the end.

"She should seriously change that," Caroline says. "Because check out the posts. I mean, she's trying to create a fresh but painfully vague new narrative, but no matter how you slice it, she clearly ain't in Hollywood no more."

In one photo, she stands before a beautiful upper-class home with a huge park-worthy fountain in front, wearing another gorgeous outfit. The caption simply reads: *Fabulous!* "That's gotta be a house her mom is trying to sell—in some upscale Louisville neighborhood and not anywhere near Sweetwater," my friend imparts.

In another, Jasmine's peeking from beneath the brim of a wide-brimmed hat you might see someone wear to the beach or...maybe an L.A. garden party. Caption: *So chic.*

In a third, she's pulled together some sort of country princess look that involves an off-the-shoulder blouse and a long side braid. It's a selfie taken at a creative angle, against the backdrop of a familiar white split-rail fence and, if I'm not mistaken, a horse named Lady Jane. The caption reads: *Kentucky Dreamin'.*

"See, here she's trying to plant the seed of travel and an unrealistically-glamorous version of Kentucky that I imagine will bring out a beyond-elaborate hat and mint julep for the derby if she's still here in May. She's trying to show her followers that she's somewhere else, without explaining why. And as for those vague, clipped captions, I think that's how the cool kids do it—to, like, imply they're just too in demand to type more. It must be so much work to orchestrate these perfect shots."

"That's at Luke's farm," I point out.

At this, Caroline gasps. She knows about the kisses that didn't quite happen. "Do you think she was at the farm *with* Luke?"

Of course, my mind went to the same place. But I answer, "In fairness, I can tell it was taken from the stretch of fence by the road, where literally anyone could stop a car and get out. And I've seen that particular horse, Lady Jane, in that same spot—so maybe she likes to hang out there. Maybe Jasmine brought an apple."

"Maybe it was *forbidden*," Caroline adds dramatically, smoky eyes narrowed in condemnation. "And she offered it to Luke, since she's still clearly trying to lure him into her clutches."

"Whatever the case, she had to be freezing in that top." I roll my eyes. "She's seriously dedicated to her craft."

That's when Geneva exits the kitchen, wiping her hands on a small towel. "If you ask me," she says, "you two should feel sorry for Jasmine." Clearly she's heard every word.

But Caroline's not having it. "*Sorry!* Are you kidding? Why would we feel *sorry* for her?"

Geneva simply shrugs. "Look at her. Not at the pictures on that phone, but at the *big* picture. You two have done exactly what you wanted with your lives, but her—she's failed. She's back in the last place she wants to be."

Caroline just sneers. "It's the last place *we* want her to be, too."

"And you know our past with her, Geneva," I remind her. "As much as I hate to admit this, every time I look at her, I'm reminded of the scared teenager I once was, who she treated like garbage. She's this beautiful, stylish, put-together woman I'll never be, who makes me see everything I'm not."

"But none of that is real," Geneva insists. "What's real is that every day you do what you love. You chose to make a life here, and you're succeeding at it. Whereas that girl is lost and alone and...well, everything you were when she made your life hell."

"Sorry, G," Caroline says, "if I'm struggling to dredge up much sympathy. She tortured us for years."

But Geneva steps up closer and persists. "The point is— you win. You win at life. Both of you. Are your lives posh and glamorous? No. But I don't believe either of you have ever wanted that because you both appreciate simpler things. She obviously works very hard trying to be happy, but she always looks angry instead. For you two, happiness comes easier. So maybe you could give her a little compassion."

Caroline and I just look at each other. I don't quite feel it in my heart, the way Geneva is suggesting, but I can't deny that she's kinda right. The one thing I do feel is... "Ugh. She's turned us into sniveling eighth graders again."

Apparently not quite ready to concede yet either, Caroline glances back to Geneva, her expression holding a challenge. "What if she steals Taylor's man again?"

At this, however, I roll my eyes. "She can't. Because he's still not my man."

"I think he *could* be. Maybe." She twists a lock of dark hair around her finger, flashing seductive eyes.

I, however, simply *whoosh* out a sigh as Geneva comes closer, switching her gaze back and forth between us.

"What don't I know about?" she asks.

"Two near-miss kisses," Caroline informs her. "One that ended up on the cheek, the other interrupted right before it happened."

Sheesh. It's not that I'm trying to keep anything from

Geneva; it's that I'm trying not to blow this out of proportion. It's that I'm confused by the situation.

But I've felt *less* confused since leaving his house the other day.

"Well," Geneva says to me with a conspiratorial grin, "it sounds like you two are picking up right where you left off all those years ago. Like romance is only a kiss away."

This, however, draws only another eyeroll from me. "Don't you guys see all the problems with this?"

Their blank-eyed stares tell me they don't.

"Okay, well, let me enlighten you. Luke is kind of…"

"A Greek god?" Caroline asks.

I never thought about it that way before, but… "Yes. Exactly. He's handsome and rugged and sporty and confident. And me, I'm still a little awkward, still that girl who acts nervous with a guy she's really into. I'm messy, not fancy. Look," I say, pointing down. "I already have a stain on my shirt and it's not even ten o'clock. I'm the girl who walks around town with flour in her hair." I keep coming back to that—I guess because it sums me up perfectly. And never fails to remind me that Luke can have any girl he wants, so even if there's a mutual attraction between us, in the end, won't I just somehow embarrass myself?

"And not only that," I add, "but he'll be leaving soon anyway. Whenever he gets his father's affairs settled and figures out what to do with the farm, he's going back to Utah."

Setting her towel aside, Geneva pulls out a chair and sits down with us, then looks me in the eye. "I've known you for a long time, honey," she says, "so I'm gonna be frank. I think sometimes you take relationships too seriously. *All* relationships. You...don't trust easily."

I tilt my head, considering her words. I can't deny their accuracy, but... "Maybe that's true. Some people make me feel safe with them—like you two. And with other people, it's different. And...maybe I don't feel safe with Luke. And it's not even his fault. For two people who grew up in the same small town, we come from different worlds. Maybe I suffered too much ridicule in front of him when we were young. Maybe I think that...if I let him get too close, he'll eventually figure out I'm not all that great."

As we sit in an almost deafening silence, I'm pretty sure my blunt honesty just sucked all the air from the room.

"Wow, that's a lot," Caroline says.

"Well, I, for one, feel better," I announce. "Because ever since Luke came home, I haven't been able to put my finger on what's holding me back with him, but I think I just did. It's all suddenly clear to me."

Across the small table, however, Geneva gives me a look and shakes her head. I feel a lecture coming on. "Listen to me, honey. Leave the past in the past. You're making this way too complicated, when it's simple. And so what that he's leaving? You ask me, that makes it even simpler. You've had a crush on that boy for as long as I've known you, and here he is, finally crushing on you, too. So you should just go for it. This is your chance to show him just how incredible you are —because whether you know it or not, you are—and while you're at it, have some fun for once in your life."

I let my eyes widen on her as I reply, "You certainly make it *sound* simple—but I'm not so sure it *feels* that way."

"Push all that past crap out of the picture," she says, "and it will."

I take a deep breath, trying to imagine that, me getting rid of past memories, past humiliations, past unanswered wishes and desires, and truly just being in the now with Luke Montgomery, for however long it lasts, come what may.

She's right—that's not how I'm wired.

But what if I were?

"Okay," I reply, "so say I take your devil-may-care advice and just 'go for it,' as you so succinctly put it. What happens when he leaves and I'm heartbroken? Or if I end up that way even before then? What if it turns into a big pile of regret?"

Geneva just smiles and, without missing a beat, answers, "I'd much rather have a pile of regrets than a bunch of what-ifs."

16

JANUARY 27

Luke

I'm in the guesthouse office on a cold, overcast day doing business. Estate business, Canyon Life business, and bank business regarding a potential horse sanctuary. I sit at Dad's desk, the top littered with insurance policies, estate papers, bank information, and notes I've written to myself. Most of the notes are about this horse park concept.

Am I really considering opening a second business eighteen hundred miles away from the first one? It sounds almost overwhelming, but it does tick a lot of boxes when it comes to doing the best thing for Sweetwater. I'm not sure if Hank at the inn will buy into it—but I'm also not yet sure the *bank* is buying into it, so first things first.

It's four days until my deadline with Northcutt, so I'm hoping to hear from the bank any minute now—but in the meantime, I'm busy keeping other plates spinning. The estate lawyer asked for some paperwork I haven't been able to find, so my next task is digging through Dad's desk drawers and file cabinet. He was resistant to digitizing things, and now I'm the one paying for it.

As I open drawers and riffle through them, I think back to that surprising talk with Mom the other day. I'm still not sure I believe any of it, and think maybe she just exaggerated it all, if only in her own memory. If there's anything about Dad and me that's actually resonated since he died, it's something Taylor pointed out—that maybe the one way we connected was through the horses. I guess that's something—even if I wish there'd been more.

All I know is, despite everything, here I am, the one stuck cleaning up the messes Dad left behind.

Finding nothing business-related in the last desk drawer, I'm about to close it—when my eyes fall on a thin green binder with *Luke* written on it in black in my dad's meticulous print. I pull it out and, underneath, lay binders bearing Tom and Aaron's names as well. What the hell have I stumbled onto?

I open mine and discover...a scrapbook?

It's not the kind with stickers or colored paper—it's just a collection of things about me.

It starts with little articles cut from the *Sweetwater Times* when I was in middle school—accounts of football and basketball games where I'm mentioned or pictured. Dad highlighted my name in each, and in that same black print, labeled them all with a date.

Turning more pages, I find the same types of things from high school, with track meets added in. I discover a picture of me as prom king from the paper, followed by my letter of acceptance into the University of Kentucky.

How is this even possible?

I'm thinking that's where it'll end, since that was pretty much the last of my local accolades—but when I flip to the next page, I'm even more shocked to find a shot of me on a horse at the ranch in Utah when I was twenty-one. Maybe I texted it to Mom. Did he actually have it printed out to put here?

After that come a few other personal photos I sent to Mom—from the ranch, or from hikes in Zion. Somehow he got his hands on an article from the *Springdale News* in Utah featuring a picture of me hiking the Narrows. And one more page turn reveals an article in the Moab paper from when I opened the second store there.

That's where it stops. It's only twenty or thirty pages of memories.

And a glance tells me that both of my brothers' are thicker—but who cares?

To think he took the time to do this, make this, astounds me.

And yeah, it's still about accomplishments—which is why my brothers' are bigger—but maybe that's the only way he knew how to measure things.

All I know is, for the first time in my life I feel...almost worthy in his eyes.

17

JANUARY 28

Taylor

The weather has been extra cold the past couple days, keeping foot traffic to a minimum in the shop, so I sent Geneva home early, leaving just me and Mags to helm the ship. No one has given her a treat for hours, a rare occurrence around here, so I reach in her jar and hand one down to her.

Then, as daylight fades to dusk, I wipe down the counter, cleaning up some crumbs, and pull a business card from the valentine box.

After which I reach for my phone. "Hank, it's Taylor from the Sweetheart Bake Shop. You're my weekly winner for a cake or pie of your choice."

"Well, that's nice to hear," he says. But he sounds like a

man parked under a perpetual black cloud whose given up hope of ever seeing the sun again. "Only good news I've had today, in fact. I'm on pins and needles wondering what Luke Montgomery is gonna do about that drywall plant? You heard anything?"

Poor Hank. "No," I say. I haven't heard from Luke at all, in fact, but I'm sure he's busy dealing with that and everything else. "It's only three days until the deadline, though, so we'll find out soon, one way or another."

"Fingers crossed I'll be using that cake to celebrate my retirement to Hawaii when we sell to Northcutt."

The very notion of the factory makes my stomach churn. "Would you really go to Hawaii, Hank?"

He lets out a resigned sigh. "Oh, probably not. Not sure *what* I'd do," he admits. "But the weather today sure makes it tempting. And it'd be nice to have the option."

"Well, you just order your cake whenever the urge strikes," I tell him.

He thanks me and we hang up—but the conversation puts *me* on pins and needles, too. For more than one reason. Sweetwater's fate. And mine—with Luke. I've been giving a lot of thought to Geneva's advice. And if I could really take it. Would it be worth it, knowing whatever happens between us is temporary?

Deciding I might as well close up for the night, I break my own rule and bend down to nuzzle my dog. "What do you think, Mags? Is some romance worth it if I end up broken-hearted afterward?" When she leans into my hand, it warms my heart. "At least I know *you'll* still love me no matter what."

When the shop door opens, I look up, then flinch. I couldn't be more stunned to find Jasmine Dupree standing before me wearing a sophisticated butter yellow pantsuit and her usual look of disdain.

She actually winces at the sight of me. "Oh, it's you."

My stomach shrivels at the awful greeting. "Nice to see you too, Jasmine."

"I didn't know you worked here."

"I own the place," I inform her.

"Oh," she replies, not sounding particularly impressed. One more put down, this one just slightly more subtle.

And to my utter surprise, my docile little dog who can't see a thing bares what are left of her teeth and begins to emit a low growl. I've never been so amused by Maggie's keen senses as in this moment, but if Jasmine notices the elderly poodle snarling at her from a few steps away, she doesn't let it show.

And as she studies the display case, that's when I ask myself: What if...? What if I weren't the girl Jasmine bullied for years? What if I were closer to being that person who stood up to her the one time I really had to, the day the valentine box was at stake? What if I didn't cower inside at her meanness? What if I just let it roll off me? What would that look like?

"Did you want something?" I ask her pointedly. "Or did you just come in to be rude?" It sounds as undaunted and self-assured as I hoped. And I *feel* a little tougher inside.

She, however, appears taken aback. Good. "My mother asked me to pick up some cupcakes for an open house tonight. I'll take half a dozen white and half a dozen choco-late," she says.

While boxing them up, I grow so bold as to ask, "What brings you back to Sweetwater?" Just to see what she says. Will she dare be honest, real, authentic? Especially since everyone in town seems to know the truth anyway? Or will her answer be Instagrammable?

"Just an extended Christmas visit home," she answers, smiling a fake smile now, like we're fake friends. Which we most certainly are not.

As the plate-glass door closes behind her a minute later, it occurs to me for the first time ever that maybe I do feel sorry for her.

18

JANUARY 30

Taylor

I'm rolling out dough in a white apron speckled with pink and red hearts when I hear the shop door open. It's early and I'm alone, so I call, "Be right there," then reach to wipe my hands on a damp towel.

That's when I exit the kitchen to find Luke Montgomery standing across the counter, as thoroughly hot and hunky as ever. I'm *so* sure I have flour in my hair. "Good morning," I say. "Sorry you caught me looking so—"

"Yummy?" he asks.

I try to suppress my reaction, but the word sends ripples of delight all through me and I'm pretty sure it's written all over my face. I walk around the display case to stand face to face with him. "I was gonna say messy, but…maybe I like your take on it better." Whoa, look at me, flirting!

He smiles into my eyes to say, "I can't stay long—tons to do—but I wanted you to be the first to know."

My heart nearly seizes in my chest. I don't have to ask what he's talking about. "What's the verdict?"

"I've just secured a loan to start a horse park and sanctuary. Mom is investing some money, too—entirely her choice. She loved the idea and offered. And she wants to be closely involved."

It's all I can do not to jump for joy. "Luke, this is amazing! What incredible news! I'm thrilled!"

So thrilled, in fact, that I impulsively throw my arms around his neck in a huge hug.

And when I realize what I've done, I experience half a second of panic and embarrassment—until his arms close warmly around my waist, and then there's nothing but the closeness of him, the hardness of his male body against my softer curves, and I forget about anything else for a long, blissful moment.

When we finally part, I go back to feeling a little embarrassed—when I see what I've left behind on him. "I got flour on you," I say softly, reaching to brush at the T-shirt he's wearing beneath an open flannel shirt. Which means I'm actually brushing his chest. Not on purpose exactly, but it's nice.

He simply casts me a cute grin. "Well worth it."

I nibble my lower lip as the heat of a blush climbs my cheek. "Tell me more," I say. "About the park, I mean."

He looks so happy that it fills me up inside—I can feel the

weight lifted just from the expression on that handsome face. "I'm calling a meeting tomorrow night at the high school to share the news, with some details, but I'm excited about the possibilities for the town. I'm thinking we can carry the horse theme right on to Main Street, with the idea of making the sanctuary and Sweetwater itself kind of synonymous—you think of one, you think of the other."

I plant my hands jokingly on my hips. "Now wait just a minute, Mr. Montgomery. *Hearts* are kind of our thing here in Sweetwater." I motion around me to the hearts all over the shop—from the ones painted on the walls to the baked ones behind glass. They happen to grace Sweet Caroline's Deli, too, and even the sign for Sweetwater Drugs.

In response, though, he takes my hand and leads me to my own door, which he opens, then glances up and down mostly-vacant Main Street. "I'm sorry to break this to you," he imparts in a kind, if teasing, tone, "but I'm not sure it's working."

"Okay," I say, smiling in concession, "I guess we can have hearts *and* horses."

As the door closes, shutting back out the cold, he asks, "How do you like the sound of the Sweetheart Horse Park and Sanctuary? If you don't mind me borrowing your name."

"I don't mind at all." In fact, it makes me even happier. Because... "It's perfect."

"This is all thanks to you, Taylor," he tells me, his smile fading to something more circumspect.

And that's when I realize we stand only a few inches apart and he's looking at me in that same way he has before, his eyes darkening with want and intention—and I'm so, so ready for it this time, finally.

He reaches for my hand and leans closer—as the front door bursts opens and I instinctively step back from him, turning to see Kyra.

She appears completely focused on her shoes as she wipes them on the heart-laden welcome mat, with no clue she's interrupted anything. "Morning. Sorry I'm late. My brother wouldn't get out of the shower." Only then does she raise her gaze. "Oh, hi. Didn't realize we had a customer. Sorry." She smiles her apology, then heads to the back, leaving us alone again.

But only until—I truly can't believe it—Jeff from the drugstore comes waltzing in. "Morning, Taylor. Think I need a cupcake to start the day. Don't tell my wife, though—she's on me about the sugar intake lately. And no rush—I need to look at the wares and decide what I'm in the mood for."

As Jeff proceeds past us to the display case, Luke grins down at me to softly say, "Foiled again. Why does this keep happening?"

"Seems like our timing is never quite right," I answer just as quietly.

This time, though, I'm not glad or relieved. This time I wanted the kiss so badly I could taste it.

Which perhaps means...I've decided Geneva is right? That I should just go for it, come what may?

"I need to take off," he tells me, apparently giving up on this for now. "But before I forget..." He steps over to insert a folded piece of paper into the valentine box.

"What's that?"

"Meeting details." He offers up another cute grin. "I know I could have just handed it to you, but for old time's sake." And with that, he heads toward the door.

"Luke," I say.

He stops, looks back.

"About our timing not being right…"

"Yeah?"

"Don't stop trying."

19

FEBRUARY 1

Luke

As people arrive at the school gym—where TJ arranged for us to meet again—I welcome them, but stay tight-lipped, because I don't want to have to explain this ten times. It's difficult, though, since I'm excited about the news. I only hope they will be, too.

Beside me stands an easel propping up a large piece of foam board—covered with a tablecloth until I'm ready to reveal what's underneath.

Soon everyone is seated on the bleachers. I've got Jasmine mooning at me from the front row in some designer dress more suitable to Beverly Hills than the Sweetwater High gymnasium. And Hank scowls at me from just behind her— he might be my toughest nut to crack here tonight. The Little

Dipper Holcumb family is here, along with Billy, Stan the Barber, Jeff from the drugstore, and others. But when I spot Taylor in her cute little *Sweetheart Bake Shop (Not a Diner!)* tee, something in my chest expands.

Maybe I'm remembering that last kiss we didn't quite have. Frustrating, sure. But the electricity that sizzled between us, the look in her eyes afterward, and that 'Don't stop trying'—it all has that same current vibrating in the air between us now, even with twenty other people here.

After I thank everyone for coming, I dive right in with, "I know you're all eager to hear what we've decided regarding the Northcutt Drywall deal. I have a lot to say, so before taking any feedback, let me fill you in on the whole picture.

"First of all, we declined the Northcutt offer." At this, a few gasps sound, and I sense mostly relief echoing through the small section of bleachers in front of me. But not from Hank—the lines etched into his weary face seem to set harder and deeper. Because it was an all-or-nothing deal, Hank told me to just agree to it or not and then let him find out along with everyone else, saying his heart couldn't take the ups and downs. But I know he was among the few hoping for a different answer.

"Obviously, it's a lot of money to pass up. And, as we discussed, an influx of traffic that would likely bring new business to Sweetwater. But no matter how Mom and I looked at it, it didn't seem right for the town or the people who live here.

"However, because we know Sweetwater definitely needs *some* kind of boost to keep it from dying completely, we're doing something else with the farm that will hopefully enhance rather than detract from the area's charm. And so I present to you preliminary plans for the Sweetheart Horse Park and Sanctuary." Like a magician in his ta-da moment, I whisk the tablecloth from my easel as another soft gasp echoes through the crowd.

"We've secured a loan to convert our family farm into a sanctuary for horses in need of rehoming or a place to retire. The business aspect of this is the park component—we'll offer rides, a horse visiting and viewing area, lectures, and more." I pick up the pointer TJ uses to explain football diagrams to his players and use it to tap my rudimentary map. "We'll build a second barn here. And a gift shop here. Over here will be a concession booth and some picnic tables. And we'll add a parking lot here.

"The hope is to make it a Kentucky destination, and in the long run, that's ultimately good for *everyone* running a business in Sweetwater." I conclude then with, "Okay, that's it. What do you guys think?"

Answers come all at once.

"No huge factory is a good thing. That plus a new draw to the area is a *great* thing."

"So happy the farm will stay!"

"What an incredible idea."

Then my mom's hairdresser, Wanda, speaks up. "How does your mother feel about this, Luke? She's just buried your father, and now her home is changing into a park?"

I give the older woman a kind smile. "I understand and appreciate that concern, Wanda, but she's all in. In fact, I suspect this project is going to become her new passion in life. We'll place a plaque memorializing Dad for first making the farm a place to provide sanctuary for horses, and she's very dedicated to honoring him that way. She has a lot of grieving to do yet—we all do. But I think this is going to be exactly what she needs."

Billy throws up a hand to ask, "How many horses are you thinking the farm can support?"

"That's a great question, Billy," I reply. "Comfortably, we can handle up to about twenty as it stands, even sacrificing a little space to the new structures and parking area. That's a dozen more than we have right now. But I would love to acquire more acreage so that we can potentially take that number higher."

"Buy *my* place," Hank yells out. "Give me fair market value and you can have the whole kit and caboodle."

I toss him a glance. "You want to talk with me afterward, Hank?"

"Ain't nothing you can say to me in private that I mind folks hearing," he shoots back.

"All right then," I answer. "I was planning to offer on about half the inn's grounds if that interests you. I'm hoping you'll stay open, though—give us a chance to get up and running—because with any luck, the park will draw some overnight visitors. It's possible we might even host a week-long horse camp for kids—with chaperones, of course—and the campers would need a place to stay. Ultimately, I think the town will need an inn again. Plus it would be a great place to hold official meetings, fundraising luncheons, things like that. But if you're still ready to shut the doors, I'll buy the inn from you, too, and make it part of the park."

I can see the wheels turning in Hank's head the whole

time I'm talking, and after a moment, he scrunches his mouth up this way and that before finally saying, "Well, if you really think people'll come, I'll try to stay open."

"Good," I reply with a smile. "The place wouldn't be the same without you."

Paul Holcumb raises his hand then to say, "Luke, I want to thank you for thinking outside the box on this. I know you gave up a big payday and could have just taken the money and run. Most people would have. I give you a lot of credit for putting the town before yourself and your family. Takes a lot of integrity to do that. And a lot of creativity and dedication to come up with a plan like this."

I give the man a solemn, grateful nod. I guess he's right, but leaving my hometown worse than I found it was a much bigger factor for me than the cash. "Well," I answer, "rest assured that it was ultimately Mom's decision and she's very happy about it. I am, too." I suffer a little pang of guilt toward Hank then, since my family is fortunate the money wasn't vital to us, but I try to push it aside since I honestly think even *he* will ultimately be happier this way.

"As for the creative aspect, I have to give credit where it's due," I go on. Then I look toward the pretty redhead in the stands. "The basic idea for changing the farm into a destination was all Taylor's. I just took it and ran with it."

Widened eyes turn in her direction with murmurings of, "Good job," and "Thank you, Taylor!"

"Oh, and one last idea—something Mom came up with just last night," I add. "We want to start an annual horse festival, something that can expand through the whole town."

Then I look back to Taylor. "I'm thinking a good name might be 'Hearts and Horses.'"

"Oh, that's cute," Janet Dupree says, apparently unaware that her daughter sits next to her flinging daggers at me with her expression. Underneath all the glitz and exaggerated confidence, Jasmine is like a little lost puppy growling at everyone she encounters. But does she truly still think there's something between us? I ignore the scowl on her face—Taylor-related, I'm assuming—and thank everyone for coming.

People seem to want to talk with me as the small crowd disperses, mostly with words of relief or gratitude—but when I spot Hank skulking toward the gym doors, I hastily excuse myself to catch up with him. "Hank," I call from a few steps behind.

He looks back.

"This is gonna be good, I promise. And like I said, if it's not, I'll make things right with you."

He appears doubtful, though. "Not as right as Northcutt was gonna make it."

He's still mired in the deflating news that he's not an instant multi-millionaire. And I get it. "Well, afraid I don't have pockets that deep. But I hope you can understand that we're trying to do what's best for the biggest number of people and work for the greater good."

The big sigh he lets out comes with a conceding nod. "Believe it or not, there's a part of me that feels the same as everybody else—glad we'll still have our pretty shoreline. I just gotta soak it all in, and...hope for the best, I guess."

"Thanks for being open to the idea."

"And I'll think about selling you some acreage."

"That sounds good, Hank—I appreciate it." I shake his hand and give his shoulder a bolstering squeeze as I send him on his way.

That's when Taylor and her friend Caroline pass me on the other side, leaving—and I don't want to let *her* get away tonight, either. "Taylor."

They both stop, and she offers up a small smile with a cute tilt of her head. "You didn't have to give me so much credit, you know. I'm just happy things are working out."

"Me, too," I say, stepping closer. And maybe I mean that in more ways than one. Coming home, I never expected the perk of reconnecting with Taylor Mulvaney. And kissing her still remains very high on my to-do list. "Hey, are you busy now? Could we go somewhere and...chat?" I really mean make out, but I'm happy to start with some chatting.

"I need to go back to the shop for a little while, but you could meet me there when you're done here."

"It's a date," I tell her.

"Um, how did I never notice this dog before?" I ask a little while later. Taylor's little white furry companion—she says it's a poodle, but it doesn't look much like one to me—walks beside her on a leash as we head toward the old Riverview Park just behind her shop on Main. We're both in our winter coats, but temps have grown unseasonably mild the last couple of days—it's in the forties, even after dark.

"Well, she's old and quiet," Taylor replies, her voice filled with affection for the pup, "which is pretty much what makes it okay for her to come to work with me. I leave her at home if it's super stormy out or something, but it makes her sad, and I like giving her as full a life as possible."

"So she can't see anything, huh?" Taylor mentioned it while leashing her up at the shop.

As we turn the corner that leads to the river, she nods. "She learned her way around my house, though, and when she's on the leash, she knows to just go straight unless I guide her to the left or right. She might be old and blind, but she's a smart girl."

"And...it's okay," I narrow my eyes on her curiously to ask, "to have a dog in your bake shop?"

"Well, since we keep her very tidy and in one area, and poodles don't shed, they let me claim she's an assistance animal." Her eyes tell me that even she knows that's a stretch, but that she's grateful for the latitude.

Our way is lit by dilapidated streetlamps that have seen brighter days, but recent snows have all melted, so the way is clear for both us and the dog as we follow Riverview Drive the short distance to the park.

"About telling everyone at the meeting the horse park was your idea," I say then, "I just thought they should know."

"All *I* know," she answers, still sounding as humble as before, "is that you made a lot of people very happy tonight, and a lot more optimistic about the future."

"Mom and I are both optimistic, too."

She looks up at me as we walk. "How did your brothers take the news?"

I tip my head back, remembering two unpleasant phone

conversations. "Not great. At first. Especially Tom." I slant her a glance. "Word of the day: *Tomfoolery*. Which is what I've been putting up with from him."

She lets out a short laugh.

"But I think, deep down, they know they can't complain too much about decisions they weren't here to help make. Not to mention decisions that make Mom happy and give her a sense of purpose. And one thing that helped, even with Tom and Aaron, was knowing how much Dad would approve."

"You know," she says, "when you mentioned a plaque honoring him, it's the happiest I've heard you sound when talking about your father...ever."

Even though I still don't like discussing my relationship with Dad, I've found Taylor easy to confide in. So I confide a little more. "My mom claims he was just bad at expressing his feelings. And...I actually found this little scrapbook he'd kept —everything from my high school sports stuff to articles about my business—and...I don't know...maybe it helped a little."

"Luke, that's great," she says, then grabs onto my hand and squeezes it.

I squeeze back and don't let go.

Taylor

And just like that, we're holding hands. When I took his, it was instinctive, purely without thought—but now I feel swept up in the simple connection, like my whole world centers on the spot between us where my hand fits into his, and nothing else matters but the ribbon of sensation fluttering up my arm and down through my body. Neither of us is wearing gloves tonight, either!

We walk in silence and my heart beats harder, merely from his touch. Does he feel it as intensely as I do? Or is that silly of me? To think a guy like Luke Montgomery, who has surely had so many more relationships than me, could be experiencing the same tingling pleasure I am, just from holding hands?

When it comes to the guys I've dated, mostly from outside Sweetwater, I usually break up with them after a month or so because I'm just not that into them. With Luke, though, every second, every sensation, is amplified. Just like in high school.

"About your dad," I say, deciding we should talk again before I get caught up in any old emotions still lingering inside me, "back at the meeting, you almost actually said you were grieving. And grieving isn't fun, but...at least it means you had something *worth* grieving, right?"

Beside me, he just shrugs, still squeezing my hand. "Guess that's true."

He still sounds a bit wooden on the topic, so maybe I shouldn't push it. But this feels like forward movement, healthier than when he came home acting like his mother was the only one who'd lost somebody.

"Speaking of things that aren't fun," he says, "this park really needs to be revamped, doesn't it?"

I glance around the narrow stretch of land behind the Main Street shops that hasn't changed much since I moved here over twenty years ago, and it was already rundown then. A shabby basketball court is missing nets and suffers from badly cracked concrete, with weeds growing up through the fissures even in winter. An old picnic shelter sports broken-down wooden tables and an ancient grill that pokes up from the ground on a rusty pole. Beyond that lies the remains of a playground that now consists only of an old swing set with just two questionable-looking swings left, and one bouncy animal on steel springs where there were once four. The survivor is so badly faded I can't tell what it originally was.

Peering at it in the glow of the streetlights, I tilt my head to ask, "Do you think this was an elephant?" I'm basing that mainly on the fact that it's gray. "Or it could be a rhino."

Luke studies it, too, finally replying, "Elephino," and I hear myself giggle, remembering the old joke: *What do you get when you cross an elephant with a rhinoceros?*

After we share a short laugh, Luke goes on about the park. "Maybe now that the horse sanctuary is in the works, the town could apply for a grant to upgrade the place. I can easily see the whole area redone. Benches along the river. A new shelter, or more than one. Maybe a walking path, and definitely a new playground. All horse-themed."

Still holding his hand, which I never want to let go of, I suggest, "Or heart-themed." Yes, he's beyond hot, and yes, I'm on board with the horse stuff, but I'm still not letting go of our Sweetwater hearts.

He turns to face me with a teasing grin. "I thought we agreed that horses and hearts could co-exist peacefully together. Maybe even complement one another. Ya know," he says, tilting his head, "sometimes two things that seem very different can go together just fine."

Like us, he means. "Maybe so," I have to agree. I always

felt our two worlds, even in the same small town, were just too far apart—but maybe that's changing.

When he releases my hand to take a seat on the elephino, I miss the touch immediately. Yet then he gazes at me from his new perch to say, "Sit down with me."

I'm about to ask where—it's definitely a one-seat animal—when he pats his knee.

Does he see me swallow past the nervous lump that's just materialized in my throat? Thank goodness the lighting from the lamps is dim at best. "That seems like...a risky proposition." Maybe for more reasons than one. But on the practical side, it's a fairly small elephino.

"Don't worry," he replies. "I've got you."

Okay then. Part of me wants to run from this moment, this invitation to intimacy—an *old* part that I understand but also want to let go of so badly. So I lower myself, slowly, gingerly, onto his lap, Maggie's leash looped around my wrist.

It's warm there, warmer than the weather should allow for, and even more so when he eases one arm around my waist, the other reaching to close over my outer thigh to hold me in place.

"We're lucky this thing hasn't gone crashing to the ground," I tell him. His strong arms support me completely and he smells like leather.

"Feels fine to me," he promises, his face near mine, voice dropping lower, eyes shaded.

And that's when he leans in to kiss me. And this time nothing interrupts us.

It's only a soft meeting of mouths that lasts a few seconds, but it oozes through me like hot lava, stealing my breath.

"I've been waiting almost fifteen years to do that," he whispers deeply.

The words increase my already-thudding heartbeat, and I whisper back, "Was it...worth the wait?"

"Oh yeah," he says. "And in fact, I'm gonna do it again."

This time it's a deeper kiss, and the sheer pleasure dissolves every ounce of nervousness inside me. Luke Montgomery is kissing me at last, kissing me the way young girls dream of. Older girls, too. And yeah, it was *so* worth the wait.

As it continues, I begin to forget about things. Where we are, that it's chilly out, that there's a dog roaming around below our feet, that we're sitting on an unrecognizable, decades-old piece of playground equipment where I'm pretty sure no one ever had as much fun as we're having right now. It consumes me.

It consumes me...except for one niggling notion. *If kissing him feels this amazing, how much is it gonna hurt when he's gone?* But I push that aside, same as yesterday, because I'm embracing Geneva's advice, right? *Have fun with him tonight and don't worry about tomorrow.*

20

FEBRUARY 2

Taylor

It's Groundhog Day and according to the news, Punxsutawney Phil predicts another six weeks of winter. But me, I couldn't care less because as I walk up Main Street toward Sweetwater Drugs, I'm still warmed by the memories of Luke's kisses last night. I lost track of how long they lasted, but we stopped only when Maggie began to whimper—her way of saying, *Let's go home*—making me feel like a bad dog mom.

"Sounds like somebody's getting impatient," he said on a sigh.

"It's past her dinnertime," I realized out loud. But I was mainly thinking how amazing it was to be that close to him, one arm looped around his neck, his face only a few inches from mine.

"I'll walk you to your car," he told me with a sexy grin.

Parting from him, physically, was harder than I could have anticipated. It felt like finally being in the place you were always meant for.

But today I'm practically floating on air. I told Caroline and Geneva a little while ago. "He kissed me," I announced over coffee at Caroline's usual table. "In Riverside Park. For a long time."

Caroline gasped, then leaned close to dreamily inquire, "How was it?"

"Best kisses of my life," I said. "Not that he had dozens of other guys to stack up against, but still. Absolutely amazing."

Wiping down the display case, Geneva was all smiles. "It's about time."

"Yes," I replied, nodding to myself. "It is. I'm only sorry it's not like that old Groundhog Day movie, that I didn't wake up this morning where I was yesterday, knowing I could look forward to it all happening again."

Geneva merely shrugged. "Maybe you can anyway."

Now I'm cheerfully delivering the cupcake Jeff just called to request I bring down since he's alone in the store today.

"Seriously, do not tell my wife," he insists as usual as I step up to the counter. As I slide the cupcake to him, he in turn slides *me* a bag of Maggie's heart-shaped doggie treats. Fairly even trade, so we don't bother with a transaction.

"You seem in a good mood today," he observes as I pluck up the bag. "Great news about Luke's decision, huh?"

"Yes, the best," I say. But I'm really thinking about kissing, of course. I may never think about anything else again.

"Way to go, coming up with that plan for the Montgomery farm."

I just give him a happy, playful shrug. "I do what I can."

Sauntering merrily out the door, doggie treats in hand, I'm taking in the sky, which somehow seems extra blue today—and were white puffy clouds *always* this pretty?—when a grating voice cuts through my bliss. "Watch out!"

I pull my gaze back down to find I've nearly collided with Jasmine on the sidewalk. Talk about a killjoy. Guess I have to think about something besides kissing, after all.

The fault is mine, and I'm actually about to say I'm sorry out of sheer habit in such moments—when she glowers at me to declare, "You're not his type, you know."

Uh oh. It's Sweetwater High all over again. My stomach roils.

Only...I'm really *not* that scared girl anymore. Somewhere along the way, things have truly changed. And I won't be mistreated any longer. "What's between Luke and me is none of your business," I tell her very calmly. "And sorry to disappoint you, but I'm no longer intimidated by you and your ugly behavior."

She blinks, the shock in her gaze telling me I've thrown her off her game. Yet she regroups with an eyeroll. "Oh my God. Could you exaggerate the past any worse? Get over it already."

As she makes a move to go past me on the sidewalk, I actually step into her path, bringing her to a halt. I refuse to be gaslighted, even by someone as self-centered and small-minded as Jasmine Dupree. "First of all, if you don't think you were ugly to me, and ugly to others, for no reason whatsoever, you're deluding yourself. Or maybe there *was* a reason." I'm actually raising my voice now, angered by the past. "You needed to feel more important than you were. So you found girls who already had a tough time fitting in and you made it tougher. And now you're *still* trying to be important, to a guy who's just not into you, and you're *still* being ugly. But we're not kids anymore, and it's not working this time."

The problem with all this is...for the entire duration of my speech, a heart floats in the sky behind her head. One of those puffy white clouds has indeed turned into a perfectly-shaped heart. And I know instantly what it's telling me: that I should be the bigger person.

The one time I stood up to Jasmine, the special box from my dad was at stake. But now, I don't need to be a mean girl just because that's what *she's* always been.

And Geneva was right—Jasmine might not know it, but I have a better life than her. In the big picture, I'm happy. Maybe I have to worry about my business, but that might change for the better soon. Maybe I don't have love, but... Luke's mouth on mine last night made it seem only a heartbeat away. And maybe I don't live in a fancy house with a fancy address, but who cares? Despite how unhappy I was to be planted in Sweetwater once upon a time, I've become a part of the place in a way I wouldn't trade.

That's when I realize she's simply standing there like a deer in headlights. And her lower lip is quivering a little. I think I've actually frightened her. And I kind of want to enjoy that—but I can't. I remember all too well what it's like to be the girl who's quivering.

"And second," I go on—more calmly again, "I *am* over it. I'm content to leave the past in the past if you can be a little nicer in the present."

She still looks frozen in place, like she doesn't know what just hit her. I barely do myself. But finally she says, in little more than a complacent whisper, "Sure. Whatever."

Wow. Jasmine Dupree just made peace with me. Kind of anyway.

I'm tempted to alert the media, but instead, I remember that I know how to be a nice person, and maybe she just doesn't, and maybe I need to show her. "Listen," I say, "it's none of my business, but...I think you're going through a hard time right now, and I truly hope things get better for you."

"I'm fine," she insists so quickly that I know it's a knee-jerk reaction.

"Okay," I say. "I'm glad. Take care, Jasmine."

And with that, I step around her and start back toward the bake shop.

"Taylor."

Stunned to hear her call my name, I stop and look back.

"Thanks," she says.

I just nod, then go on my way.

She and I will never be friends. But it feels shockingly nice to walk away no longer enemies.

21

FEBRUARY 3

Taylor

The bake shop's deadline for orders to be delivered by Valentine's Day is the ninth—and they're suddenly pouring in. Like in almost overwhelming numbers. Which is great—but also stressful.

When my phone buzzes with a text, I make a face. I'm up to my eyeballs in dough here, both hands immersed in it.

Out front, we suddenly have more foot traffic than usual, and I hear Maggie barking hello to someone. Some of the customers are placing orders for pickup on the thirteenth or fourteenth; others are simply grabbing cookies or a pie to go. School just let out and three booths are filled with teenage girls snacking on cupcakes while they finalize plans for the sweetheart dance—these days held in the ballroom at the Sweetwater Inn, and one of Hank's bigger annual events.

Kyra handles the front, keeping the display case stocked while Geneva and I work in back. I'm prepping cookie dough to be stored in the walk-in freezer for use on holiday orders in the week ahead while she bakes cupcakes for the coming days.

"I figured it out."

Geneva and I both look up from our work to see Kyra's face in the pass-through window.

"Figured what out?" I ask.

"Where the extra uptick in orders is coming from." Business always increases this time of year, but we've gotten twice the amount expected by this date. Right after my run-in with Jasmine yesterday, I came back to find the orders piling up.

I let my eyes go wide. "Where?"

"Remember those two ladies you mentioned? The ones asking about the horse farm?"

"Mmm hmm." They changed the course of Sweetwater's future, so I remember them well.

"One of them is actually a famous artist—a painter—with a few hundred thousand followers on social media. And she recommended us! With a link and everything."

I'm pretty sure my jaw just dropped. First thought: "That's amazing." Second: "My God, I hope we can fulfill all the orders."

"Don't you worry," Geneva says from next to the big mixer where she's adding ingredients for chocolate cake. "We'll work around the clock for the next week if we have to. Won't we, Kyra?"

Kyra looks a little surprised by the suggestion, but then nods. "Of course. Whatever you need, Taylor."

I let out a sigh. "You guys are the best."

When my phone buzzes again, I finally take a moment to wipe my hands on my apron and look.

The first text is from my mom, offering to come up and help bake. Clearly Geneva has kept her informed on the latest. I type back: *Swamped and will take you up on it. Call you later to strategize.*

The next is from Luke. *Word of the day: Dinner? At the Big Dipper? Would love to take you someplace nicer, but since it's the only place in town...*

I let out a sad sigh. Then type out my reply. *Wish I could. But even busier than yesterday.*

He suggested getting together then, too.

I follow that with another text. *Found out someone recommended us online. Which is awesome if I can fill the orders in time. Wish I could see you, but I'll be here late again.*

Does it kill me to actually turn him down? Of course. Especially given how much our time together on the elephino has stayed on my mind.

But I have to be a responsible businesswoman. Not just for me—I employ people, and I have shop bills to pay. If money is coming in, I have to be grateful and put in the hours to keep my customers happy and hopefully coming back.

I'm really sorry, I say in one more text.

More than words can adequately express.

22

FEBRUARY 5

Luke

Rather than text her, tonight I call. For reasons both altruistic and selfish. A person can't work around the clock the way she has the last few days—she needs a break. And ever since we made out on the elephino, I've been dying to do it again. Make out, that is—with or without the elephino actually being present. I think about her constantly, and I guess maybe our timing is *still* off, but now that I've finally experienced just how good it can be between us, I'm not gonna let that stand in our way.

After five rings, she picks up. "Luke," she says, sounding harried. "Sorry it took so long to answer. I was getting pies out of the oven."

"Let me take you for a burger," I say, cutting to the chase.

She sounds tired, replying, "You have no idea how good that sounds to me right now. But there's so much to do. I'm too busy."

I'm about to answer when I hear Geneva, who I remember as a waitress from back in the day, say, "Are you really *that* busy? That you can't take an hour for yourself when a handsome man wants the pleasure of your company?"

Taylor's sigh is loud enough to hear over the phone. "You've seen all the orders. Those have to be my top priority right now. February sustains us for the rest of the year as you well know. And if we can get all these orders filled and I don't have to start issuing refunds, maybe making ends meet this year won't be as challenging as usual." Then she finally addresses *me*. "Did you catch all that?"

"I did," I tell her.

"So you get it, right? *You're* a business owner. You understand."

I hesitate just briefly before informing her, "To tell you the truth, I've never had a run on hiking equipment or mountain bikes that kept me at the shop late, and our hiking excursions sell out all the time, but that's because we put a limit on them. Which...maybe you should consider doing at this point?"

"No way," she insists without missing a beat. "Every one of these orders could turn out to be a loyal customer. I can't afford to sacrifice this opportunity."

"Okay," I answer. "And I do understand. But...remember when you told me to keep trying."

"Yeah."

"Well, that's probably gonna happen with this, too."

On the other end of the line, she lets out another sigh, but this one sounds more dreamy than frustrated. "You're sweet."

"Don't let it get around," I tease.

An hour later, I walk into the Sweetheart Bake Shop. It's after seven and the dining area is empty, but I can tell the kitchen is hopping. When a harried but gorgeous redhead pops her face up into the window, I can't help but smile.

"What are you doing here?"

I shrug. "I figure if you can't beat 'em, join 'em. I'm here to help. I know zero about baking, but put me to work however you can."

She leaves whatever she's doing and comes out behind the counter. That's when my eyes drop to the valentine box, sitting in front of her with its lid off. "What's happening here?" I ask.

"I got sidetracked. I took a few minutes about an hour ago to do my weekly drawing, but the phone rang and I never came back to it." She holds out the box. "Would you like to do the honors, sir?"

I put my hands up in a backing-off motion, and say teasingly, "I don't know—that's kind of a big responsibility."

She just shakes the open heart-shaped box in my face and I can see I'm wasting the time of a busy lady. So I draw out a card and read it. "Billy Finch."

"Excellent," she says.

"I'll let him know," I tell her. "Save you one little task."

"Thank you. I'm actually a day late drawing it. Usually, I do it like clockwork."

I nod. "Kyra told me you go through it a lot."

She blushes, just a little. "Almost daily. I don't know why. Something about it comforts me."

"I'm sure it keeps you feeling connected to your dad," I say—then I look around. "What can I do to help?" And when I realize maybe it's a tall order finding a baking job for a guy with no kitchen skills, I drop my gaze to Maggie, who has her front paws up on her gate, wanting attention. "Does the dog need walked?"

Taylor's pretty green eyes go wide. "Oh, would you? Because she totally does! I'm being a bad dog mom again."

"I don't think you could be a bad dog mom if you tried," I inform her, after which I lean across the counter, lift her chin with one bent finger, and lean in for a quick kiss.

"Oh, that was nice," she says. It comes out in this really innocent way I feel in my gut. I'm not sure she's been kissed a lot. And I'm glad to be the guy changing that.

When I come back from walking Maggie down to the park, I've made a decision. After returning the dog to her gated area, I enter the kitchen to find three women up to their elbows in flour and dough and cookie sheets and cupcake pans. "I have an announcement to make," I declare. "I'm sorry if this leaves you ladies short-handed, but I'm taking Taylor for a burger."

"Thank God," Kyra says. "She's driving us crazy."

Taylor spins to gape at her, a heart-shaped cookie cutter in her hand.

"And your mother will be here in the morning," Geneva adds. "That'll be a whole extra set of hands. We'll get caught up in no time. And you need a break. Kyra and I will finish up what's already in progress, then lock up for the night."

Taylor glances toward the front of the shop. "But—Mags."

Geneva marches over to her, a chocolate-spattered apron covering her pink T-shirt. "Give me the key to your house."

"But—"

"Give. Me. The key. She'll be there waiting for you when you get home. Probably fast asleep. Now go. The both of you. Let Kyra and me have a little peace for the first time in three long days."

Taylor's eyes go wide. "Well, if that's how ya feel..."

"We do," Geneva confirms. "Off with you now." She follows the demand with shooing motions.

"You heard the lady," I tell her, ushering her from the kitchen with a hand at the small of her back. "Let's get outta here."

"But I'm a mess," she turns to argue.

"A *gorgeous* mess," I say, after which I hear the other two cooing over that in back. I'm pretty sure they're on my side.

After she digs in her purse and delivers a key to Geneva, who followed us to the front, she reaches for her coat on a hook—as Geneva says, "Apron."

"Huh?"

"Take off your apron."

Glancing down at herself, she rolls her eyes and says, "Okay, you guys are right. I do need a break."

When we arrived at the Little Dipper, Paul was just about to close up early, but he insisted on grilling us a couple burgers. I tried to let him off the hook, but he wasn't hearing it.

Now we sit in my dad's big GMC Tahoe with the engine running, eating our hamburgers, a too-big-for-two-people basket of fries on the console between us. Paul is gone and the lot is empty, so I've positioned the SUV toward the river, where a ribbon of moonlight shimmers on the water in the distance.

"Thanks for talking some sense into me," she says between bites. "I got a little overwhelmed with all the orders. I'm excited about them, and want to make sure we get them all done. But you and Geneva are right—Mom is coming to help, and it'll be okay."

"Getting away from work is good for your sanity," I tell her. "Thank God I have the horses—and, lately, you—to get my head out of all the other stuff I'm juggling. Between dealing with my own business remotely, working on estate issues, dealing with the Northcutt decision, and now getting plans in place for a horse sanctuary..." I stop, run my hand back through my hair. "It's a lot."

"It *is* a lot," she agrees. "In fact, when you put it that way, it makes my cookies and cakes sound like nothing."

"I'm quick to shake my head. "No, we've *both* got a lot to deal with right now."

"Well," she says with a glance in the general direction of the farm, "your dad would be very proud of you for handling it all so well."

Letting that sink in, I blow out a sigh. "You know, ever since I found that scrapbook, it's had me thinking...maybe I should have come home more often. Maybe we could have had a better relationship if I'd tried harder."

The fry between her fingers goes still in mid-air, then she turns toward me in the shadowy confines of the vehicle. "Know what I think?" she begins. "That it's the parent's job to take those steps. I'm sorry he never did. But you've done nothing wrong."

Given that I've never talked much about my dad to anyone other than to gripe, she makes it easy. And so I tell her the other thing that's been eating at me the last few days. "It's almost harder finding out he cared and didn't show it than when I thought he just didn't give a damn. Does that make any sense?"

"Of course," she says. "It means you have more to mourn now. I think you just have to make peace with the fact that your relationship wasn't perfect."

"Far from it," I mutter.

"But there was still love, right? From him. From you. That's what matters."

Her words seem to reach down inside me, like something is squeezing my heart. "How did you get so wise?" I ask.

She simply shrugs, reaching for her cup in the drink holder. "Guess I've had a long time to analyze loss."

Back when we were kids and her dad died, I simply had no idea what she was going through. "You're the only person my age I know who's lost a parent," I tell her now. "I can't imagine how you coped that young. You and he were close, right?"

She nods. "I coped because there was no alternative, that's all. And this may sound silly, but...I've always felt like he's still with me."

"Not silly," I answer softly. I'm not sure what I believe when it comes to an afterlife, but I guess I've heard enough people talk about feeling the presence of a lost loved one that I don't question the validity of it.

"And..." She stops, and I can tell by her expression that she's about confide something personal. "You might think this is crazy, but...my father used to see hearts in things—in clouds or leaves or stains – anything. And he would point them out to me. And now *I* see them, too—and it always feels like they're from him."

"Not crazy," I whisper, touched that she trusted me enough to tell me.

She's looking at me, and I'm looking at her, and we both seem to be done eating, so I follow the urge to lean over and kiss her. Even after burgers and fries, like the other night, she somehow tastes as sweet as the pies and cakes she makes, like maybe all the sugar and butter are just a part of her now.

Sensation skitters down through me, warming me up from the inside out. But the big console digs into my rib, and when I shift, my elbow almost ends up in the ketchup next to the leftover fries.

I pull back with a groan, then commence loading the ketchup and leftover food into the paper sack it came from as I announce, "This console is seriously in the way."

After that, I move my seat back as far as it'll go, cast an inviting gaze to the woman across the car from me, and use my index finger to silently say, *Come here.*

She appears shy and skeptical. "Is there room?"

I give her a little grin. "More than on the elephino, and we made that work just fine."

"All right," she whispers, looking more comfortable with the idea as she carefully makes the climb onto my lap, fitting there nicely between the steering wheel and my body, her back to the door.

There are so many things I could say to her right now, about the past, about the present, about how much I wish I'd found a way to connect with her all those years ago. But we're both tired, for different reasons, and mostly, I just want to kiss her. So, lifting one hand to her cheek, that's what I resume doing.

I've kissed plenty of girls in my life and something about this one is...different, better. I feel it in my gut, not to mention other key places. Maybe because I had to wait so long? But no matter the reason, our chemistry is off the charts.

And it's more than chemistry. It's...history. And that...I *know* her. I haven't known the *adult* her long, but she's the same sweet girl as always, only stronger and more self-reliant now, more accomplished. There's not a fake or pretentious bone in her body. She's just the real deal—she's cute, quirky, sometimes-a-little-nervous Taylor Mulvaney and I wouldn't change a thing about her.

And...I want more. More than kissing. As we shrug free of our coats and I run my hands over her body, I want to touch her everywhere. As I lower my mouth from her lips to her neck and she lets out the sexiest little sigh I've ever heard, I want to *kiss* her everywhere, too.

It would be so easy. To take this farther, to indulge my every desire with her.

Except for one thing.

This isn't the time or the place. She deserves better than a backseat—or front seat—romp.

And sure, I could ask her to take me home with her tonight, but again, is this the time? When we're both exhausted and she's got an early morning? A younger me might be selfish enough to try, but the more mature Luke Montgomery knows a little patience will be worth it in the end.

Raising back up to face her, I lean over, letting our foreheads touch. The heat moving between us is almost palpable. Trying to calm it down, I find myself lifting one finger, wrapping one of those red ringlets around it, just quietly drinking her in, soaking up the nearness, the moment.

"This is nice," she whispers. Her palm presses against my chest and I wonder if she feels my heart racing.

"It is," I murmur against her hair.

We sit like that for a few minutes that are somehow at once serene and intense. Finally, I whisper, "If we stay like this much longer, I'm not gonna wanna let you go home without me tonight."

She lifts her eyes to mine, our gazes locking. Temptation simmers in hers...mingled with what I know we both feel. The reality and maturity of wanting to make it right when it happens. "Me neither. So maybe..."

It's so hard to do this, to stop this. But I care for her. And

I want to give her everything she deserves. "Maybe we should both head home?" I rasp, my voice thick with the desire I'm struggling to push down. "Let you get some rest?"

She gives me a slow, solemn, almost sexy nod. "There'll be other nights."

Oh yeah. There definitely *will* be.

23

FEBRUARY 6

Taylor

I spend the next morning at the shop wishing I could talk to Caroline about what happened with Luke last night, but we're just too busy.

In fact, my generous BFF offers to work the front counter for a couple of hours so the rest of us can focus on order fulfillment. Mom has joined our merry band of bakers, and there's much talk of "How was your little outing with Luke last night?" and "You owe us the full scoop," and then Mom asking, "What on earth have I missed?"

And it's fun and girly to talk and giggle about it as I play coy and refuse to give too much away while we all mix and stir and cut and pour. But inside, I'm brimming with emotions.

"I'm just glad you came to your senses about that boy and decided to have some fun while he's here," Geneva says as I'm sliding trays of heart cookies into the big oven. "It doesn't have to be forever to be worthwhile."

And I love Geneva, but sometimes I wonder if we're just not all wired exactly the same, if one person's fun might be another person's kryptonite. Because what I felt with Luke last night simply...isn't something I can easily let go of.

A little while later, just before Caroline leaves for the deli, she pulls me aside to echo Geneva's sentiment. "I'm so proud of you, girl," she says. "Just going for it with Luke after all this time. Not worrying about the future. Not worrying about what comes next."

I'm about to contradict the point when she throws her arms around me in a little hug and says, "See ya later—off to make the sandwiches!" And then she's gone, out the door, leaving me to wonder why I feel bad inside instead of good, and if there's just something wrong with me.

After all, Caroline dates multiple guys at once and seems to know exactly how to have fun with it and never get hurt. For a girl who grew up being called horrible things like "chunky monkey" and "wide load Loder," she's always completely in control of her life and her romantic relationships.

But then the ding of an oven timer yanks me back into the business of baking.

I'm practically knee-deep in pink frosting twenty minutes later when my phone buzzes with a text. Wiping my hands on my apron, I pull the phone from my pocket and find a text from Luke.

Dropping paperwork at the lawyer's office up the street from you at noon, so how about lunch? The deli? Won't keep you long, promise. Breaks are good, remember?

"Is that from *him?*" Mom asks. I peek over to see her raising her brows and making googly eyes in my direction. She's so happy for me. And I haven't had a chance to explain to her how my stomach churns with that weird mix of thrilling desire and nearly-paralyzing worry.

I nod. "He asked me to lunch at Caroline's."

"And you're going," Geneva chimes in without missing a beat.

Yet I hesitate. "I feel bad leaving you guys again this soon. I mean, *you* aren't going on lunch dates."

"None of us have a hot guy asking us to," Kyra points out.

"And you deserve this," Mom adds with a loving smile. "Go have fun."

There's that word again—*fun*. Everyone keeps saying it, like human connections don't matter, like you don't miss someone when they go away, like people don't form attachments with each other. But rather than say any of that, I just quietly tell them, "Okay."

Because of course I want to see him. Of course the very notion sets my skin tingling and my heart pounding. So I try to stop *thinking* and *feeling* so much and text him back. *Okay, noon at Caroline's.*

And when it's five 'til and I excuse myself from the kitchen, I lecture myself: *It's just fun, that's all. You're having fun. Like everyone says.*

And...it *is* fun. It's fun to be wooed. It's fun to feel like I have a boyfriend, even though it's extremely unofficial and temporary. It's fun to go on an impromptu lunch date. And God knows it's fun—more than fun—to exchange steamy kisses with the hottest guy I've ever known, the same guy I spent years of my life falling asleep dreaming about.

I've taken off my apron and am reaching for my parka when a striking periwinkle sweater draws my gaze out the window, across the street in front of the deli. Jasmine is wearing it—and she's talking to Luke.

My stomach ties itself in a knot as she smiles up at him and...whatever he's saying to her, he places a hand on her shoulder to deliver it.

It's dumb that my stomach hurts; it's silly that I'm flashing back to that night when they sat in one of the booths I now own, hanging all over each other while giving me dirty looks. This is...nothing. A conversation.

Except...what if I'm wrong and it's *something*? I felt like such an idiot that night, both hurt and humiliated in ways I couldn't even fully understand, and it's a way I never want to feel again.

But stop it. He's just talking to her. He's too nice to ignore her, same as when he told me she texted him. And...he owes me nothing. Certainly he can talk to whoever he wants on the streets of Sweetwater.

That's when she reaches up to touch his hair. *I want to kill her.* And—oh. His sandy hair is actually shorter than it was just last night. He's mentioned wanting to give Stan some barber business, so he must have worked that into his outing just now. I didn't think it was possible for him to be more handsome, but I was wrong.

I'm relieved when he steps quickly back from her,

though, and even more relieved when they part ways a moment later and she proceeds up Main as he steps into Sweet Caroline's.

Or...am I? I'm glad she's gone, but why do I still feel so uneasy? Clearly, old insecurities are still flaring.

But it's not about Jasmine exactly. I mean, I detest her having the nerve to touch his hair, but don't I know that, realistically, there's nothing lingering between them?

In my heart, yes.

But there's something else in my heart, too. Something big.

I'm not sure I ever stopped loving him.

Which means...I think I truly loved him back then.

Sure, I didn't know him well or spend a lot of time with him—but I fell in love anyway. He was this perfect, unattainable guy. And now I've started to know him in a deeper way and...it's made me fall in love all over again.

My heart is clearly getting wrapped up in him in a dangerous way. Like if I look out the window and see him talking to his old girlfriend and it feels like an arrow piercing my chest—and not the Cupid kind—isn't that a bad sign?

Despite what everyone thinks I'm *supposed* to feel, this isn't just fun. I'm in too deep, just as I feared.

So what am I gonna do now?

Well, in the short term, I guess I'll cross the street and have lunch with him. So I bolster myself and make my way to the deli, greeting him with a smile.

He's snagged us a table. And when I wave to Caroline, who's busy helping another customer, her eyes widen upon realizing a date is taking place before her very eyes—one more person who's so happy for me without understanding how I really feel.

And I don't even want to tell her the truth anymore, because I *want* to be this carefree, happy-go-lucky woman they all want me to be. I *wish* I were that woman. I'm just not.

Ten minutes later, I sit across from him nibbling on a hot ham and Swiss while he bites into a Reuben. He's asking how the baking is going and talking about his day, starting to sound pretty overwhelmed himself actually.

"To tell you the truth," he says, "I'm struggling with how to divide my time. Fortunately, Canyon Life isn't requiring too much input from me, but between the mountain of tasks for Dad's estate and trying to make some inroads on the horse sanctuary, I barely know which end is up. The estate business is more pressing, but at the same time, I'm eager to get construction plans in place for the new barn and other structures, plus start getting the word out because we have extra stalls already and could easily take on a few more horses as early as...today."

"So," I venture cautiously, "how will all this work? With you in Utah." And as the question leaves me, I realize it's the thing I've avoided asking—up to now.

And for a fraction of a second, I envision him telling me he's decided he wants to stay here, that things have changed for him. That connecting with me has changed *everything*.

But instead he answers, "I'll be putting together a staff. Finding some good, knowledgeable horse people and an experienced admin person. Then I'll come back a few times a year to deal with any necessary business and make sure everything's running smoothly. Plus Mom will be right on the premises, so I can get updates directly from her. I'm thrilled she'll have something good to focus on now that Dad's gone."

"Ah," I say as my heart sinks. "That sounds like a great plan."

I've been so naïve. I've known all along he wasn't staying, of course. But maybe I thought the horse park might actually draw him home for keeps. Or...maybe it just didn't matter as much until I felt us barreling toward a more intimate place last night.

When my phone buzzes, I glance down to see a text from Kyra. *We're watching you through the window.*

I look over to see three smiling faces indeed spying on us across the street through a plate-glass storefront. They think they're being funny. But I'm not amused. My heart is shriveling in my chest. And I need them busy baking, not playing games.

I use the text as an excuse. "Baking emergency," I announce to Luke.

He looks up from his sandwich, blue eyes wide. "Huh?"

"I have to go." I get up, grabbing my coat from the back of my chair.

He motions to my ham and cheese, clearly caught off guard. "You haven't even eaten."

Coat on now, I snatch up the sandwich in one hand and my fountain drink in the other. "Have to do it on the go. Sorry."

I dash away before he can even say goodbye.

24

FEBRUARY 7

Taylor

I've just finished boxing up cookies for a post office run —and breathing a big sigh of relief. The orders have leveled off even though it's two days before our Valentine's Day deadline. I guess the social media post recommending us has run its course. I'm grateful for the business, but also happy to know we'll be caught up and back to normal soon, and that we pulled it off.

The rest of the crew is baking like mad this morning as I handle the front. We'll stay busy between now and the fourteenth, but things suddenly seem back under control. Mom is working with us through tomorrow, but then I'm sending her home to David in Louisville.

Every time the shop door opens, I fear it's Luke. I'm still wild about him, but I feel a little lost right now and like I have a lot of thinking to do. Fortunately, since the moment I ran out of the deli like a woman on fire, he's only texted.

And I've done that thing where you take a while to answer, to let the guy know he's not your top priority. And since he knows I'm busy, he hasn't overdone it.

Then, however, as if the very thought conjured him, my phone buzzes, and I almost know it's him before I even look.

Glad your emergency the other day turned out to be a false alarm. (I told a little white lie to cover up my first little white lie. Even though I hate lying to anyone about anything.) *Hope things are under control.*

Of course, my first instinct is to be responsive, to tell him the mad rush is coming to an end, to finally celebrate my success a bit.

But I don't. Even if it still gives me a little thrill to hear from him, to know he's thinking about me. My confusion runs thick.

Another text rolls in, also from the man of my dreams who I'm avoiding. *I know you're still busy, but lunch at Caroline's today? Maybe you could actually eat this time.* He ends with a wink emoji.

I take a few minutes, straightening the wares in the display case. I would love to see him. In fact, I would love to let myself do everything I've ever wanted to with him.

But I'm trying to think "big picture" here. I'm trying to makes sense of the "fun" I'm supposed to be having with him, and puzzling through how "fun" could make someone this miserable. Still peering down at his name on my phone, I murmur, "You're so much more than fun."

"What?" Kyra asks from behind me.

I flinch. "Nothing," I say, trying to sound like my usual, cheerful self.

Then I text Luke back. *Sorry. Wish I could. But can't.*

25

FEBRUARY 8

Taylor

I've insisted Geneva and Kyra take a proper lunch break while Mom and I hold down the fort. Fresh-baked cakes and pies and cookies have the shop smelling even more delectable than usual as I pack up orders, stacks of pink boxes piled high around me. When my phone buzzes, it's a text from Luke.

Heard from Caroline you're getting caught up. Was thinking we could drive to Madison, go out to dinner. You need a break. We both do.

I pull in my breath. It's tempting. A real date with him. Madison is a cute town, much bigger than Sweetwater, half an hour down the river on the Indiana side, boasting quaint eateries and art galleries. It's basically everything Sweetwater would love to be.

But I text back another white lie, something I'm apparently getting good at. *Catching up, yes. But still super busy until V Day. Sorry.*

"Why does my girl look so sad?"

Just like when Kyra snuck up on me yesterday, I'm startled, and turn to find my mom—appearing concerned in that way only a mother can.

"Right when I'd think you'd be happy," she goes on. "After all, business is booming. And more will come with the horse park. Things are turning around for Sweetwater. And you're being romanced by the guy you've always wanted." She stops, giving her head a worried tilt. "You've seemed...off the last few days, but I've been chalking it up to stress. Now I'm not so sure. What am I missing?"

The truth is, I can't believe I've kept it from her so long. We've always been close, even since she moved to Louisville. I tell her everything, and she's always supportive. When I wanted to buy the diner despite it not making great business sense, she supported me. Every time I've found myself dating someone I'm not really into and announced I was ending it, she supported me. So it's probably high time I talk to her about this, too.

"It's about Luke," I say.

She lets out a sigh. "I suspected as much. What's going on?"

How do I explain this? "I love being with him, and he seems super into me. But he's leaving soon." I make eye contact with her for that last part.

"*How* soon?"

"Undetermined," I say. "But probably within another month or two. Which seems like just enough time…to get my heart broken. So I'm thinking it's a bad idea to keep going down this path."

We've both stopped working, and now she reaches out to squeeze my hand. "I understand the fear," she tells me, "but isn't it worth the risk to have the fun? You seem crazy about him, and you've wanted something with him since high school."

"*Fun,*" I spit back at her like it's a dirty word. "Everyone keeps telling me I'm supposed to be having *fun*. That I'm supposed to be all right with knowing it's casual and temporary. That I'm supposed to be able to control whether or not I get attached to a guy who's leaving. Like it's just a big game."

And as I'm telling her all this, something entirely unexpected happens: I experience a sudden burst of clarity.

Maybe it just took saying the whole thing out loud. But regardless, I keep going, telling her what I've finally just figured out. "And you know what? It's okay that I don't want that. People are always trying to push you toward casual relationships—but those don't work for everyone. I *can't* keep it casual. We have too much history.

"And do I really think this guy, this handsome hunk of man, feels anything for me like what I'm starting to feel for him? If he did, he wouldn't be planning on leaving, would he? So I think that answers that.

"Furthermore, I've forced myself into trying to be okay with *fun,*" which I still say like it's the worst thing imaginable, "because I've always been so insecure. I've always wanted to just fit in, be normal, be what everyone *thinks* is normal. But I'm being brave enough right now to say, 'No, this *fun, temporary* romance isn't for me.' And *that*, I think, is the act of a person truly secure with herself."

After all this, I blow out a breath. "Besides, it's still busy season and I have a bake shop to run."

When I meet Mom's gaze, I can tell she's hurting for me. She sees that *I'm* hurting. And that I'm protecting myself because it's what makes the most sense to me. She finally says, "Well, that's a lot to absorb."

"Are you going to argue with me about it the way Geneva or Caroline would?"

She shakes her head. "No. I trust you to know what's right for you."

Then she pulls me into a hug, which I instantly realize I need.

"I just hope you're right," she says, still embracing me. "Because...well, aren't you going to end up hurt anyway? Aren't you suffering already?"

I draw back just enough to nod—and add, "But if it went further, it would be worse. Walk away now and at least I'm ending it on my own terms."

And who knows—maybe it's a lot simpler than everything I just said. Maybe what it boils down to is that I just don't want to end up that same lonely, broken girl again, wondering why she ever gave her heart to Luke Montgomery.

Luke

Catching up, yes. But still super busy until V Day. Sorry.

I look at the words on the screen, but they don't ring true. *Nothing* about our recent communication has rung true. It grinds my heart to pieces, but I just set the phone aside and resume studying the list of contractors I'm requesting bids from for the farm expansion.

When the phone buzzes again, I'm foolish enough to let hope rise inside me in case she's changed her mind or has something a little more encouraging to say. Instead, though, it's only Hank, confirming our meeting this afternoon.

See you then, I text back. But damn, good thing he reached out, because I'd completely forgotten. We're supposed to walk his grounds and come to an agreement on how much land he's selling us.

Whatever's going on with Taylor has me off my game at a time when I can't afford to be. I've got a lot of plates to keep in the air. But this most recent rejection has me more deflated than the rest—because maybe I'm finally catching on.

Once upon a time I stood outside a gym and waited for her—only to end up feeling more rejected than ever. I have no idea how we went from talking and kissing in the car outside the Little Dipper to *this*—and it's killing me. But maybe this time I'll just take the hint and move on.

26

FEBRUARY 10

Luke

The cemetery feels stark and cold when I pull in. It's February, I know, but would it be too much to ask for a little blue peeking through the clouds? It's stayed gray and overcast the last few days, kind of like my mood.

The last time I was here, we were burying my father. I was wrapped up in comforting my mom, playing host to the crowd that followed us from the funeral home to the gravesite, and just going through all the motions as I tried to get through a tough day.

I thought it was tough because I was worried about Mom and I already knew the executorship was getting dropped on me, throwing a big wrench into my life when I least expected it. But only now can I recognize that it was tough in other ways, too. Because my dad was gone. Because I loved him even though I was mad at him for most of my life up to now.

So that day I failed to get a good look at the headstone he and Mom had already put in place a few years back. Now I take in both their names, and the peaceful image of a horse in a meadow they had engraved on it, which seems even more relevant now than they could have known then.

Mom asked me to bring some flowers for the vases on both sides of the stone, certain the live ones left behind from the funeral were long since dead and picked up by now. She just isn't ready to come herself yet. And she was right—the grave is bare and a little lonely-looking, so the bundles of red silk roses she sent me to tuck into the vases help a lot.

I'm about to leave, but then I don't. It feels like too quick of a visit, like maybe I'm supposed to be more...reverent of his resting place or something. I guess a lot has changed since he died. Back then, I refused to acknowledge I had anything to grieve. Now I know I do, and I'm just beginning to mourn the relationship we never quite had.

Maybe all of that has me wishing I could say some things to him I never got to. And whereas I don't usually talk to pieces of stone, I'm alone here, so...hell, why not?

Peering down at his name again, I begin softly, "I'm sorry we weren't closer. I could have done more as an adult to make that happen. But you could have done more when I was a kid.

"I craved your approval, but never got it. I always felt like the black sheep of the family just because we didn't care about the same things. But I'm trying to remember good times we had together. I'm grateful we had some. I'm grateful we shared a love of horses. Those really *were* our best times." I'd never thought about that until Taylor pointed it out, but she was spot on.

"You'd like what we're doing with the farm. I only wish you could see it when it's done." Then I tilt my head, remembering Taylor saying she feels like her dad is still with her. "Who knows," I go on. "Maybe you will. I don't know how things like that work, but...I hope so."

And then the damnedest thing happens. A breeze draws my gaze upward, and I notice a gray cloud darker than the rest. And...it seems almost shaped like a galloping horse.

It only lasts a second—the clouds are shifting and moving, and if there was a horse in the sky or if I just created it out of some kind of subconscious wishful thinking, it's gone before I can examine it any closer. And then it begins to snow.

When I hear a vehicle somewhere behind me, I turn and glance across the cemetery to see an SUV that looks like Taylor's—and even though it's probably seventy-five yards away, there's no mistaking the redhead who gets out and walks to a nearby grave marker that surely bears her dad's name.

I've been trying not to think about her, but it doesn't work. Either I'm reminiscing about conversations we had or I see something random that reminds me of her—someone with red hair, a poodle, a cake. *Pretty bad when a simple cake—any cake—has you thinking about the girl who clearly doesn't want you anymore.* I blow out a discouraged sigh at the thought.

And when I remember kissing her, I just don't understand how I misread her so badly. Or why she's suddenly pushing me away.

So, in closing, I take a last glance at Dad's grave and murmur, "There's this girl I like. A lot. I think she's done with me, though. It sucks. But I guess there's no time like the present to find out for sure."

And with that, I zip up my coat to ward off the wet snow and make my way toward her.

Taylor

Every February I change out the silk flowers on my dad's headstone for a bouquet of wooden hearts I bought at a craft store the year after he died. They get weather-worn, but like the valentine box, I just repaint them.

I normally come sooner in the month, but it's been an unusual February, in more ways than one. And as I lower the heart bouquet into the vase, I realize one of those ways is walking right toward me.

I guess it was inevitable to run into him again. I only hope my heart can take it. As always, the very sight of him makes my skin tingle.

"Come here often?" he asks by way of greeting. Then he lets out a cynical-sounding laugh. "That sounded more like we're in a pickup bar than a cemetery, didn't it?"

I'm tempted to tell him I wouldn't know. Maybe he goes to pickup bars. I don't. It just reminds me of what different lives we've led, and for all I know, he has a girl in every town.

The thought bolsters my decision even as I say, kindly, "Yeah, actually, I do come here a lot."

"It's my first time," he tells me. "Since the burial, I mean."

"How are you doing with it? Is it hard to be here?" I don't mean to make meaningful conversation, but despite myself, I care.

"It's...okay," he answers with a sad sort of smile. "Maybe I'm finally starting to work through the loss. You helped me with that."

I just nod. I want to say more—because I still find him easy to be with. Even if I kind of hate that now. But I stay quiet, not wanting to send mixed messages.

"By the way," he says, changing course, "some good news for you. Jasmine is leaving town."

How do you know that? Where is she going? Utah? I simply say, "Oh?"

"I saw her one day on the street and she told me she might be relocating to New York. I didn't ask for details, but yesterday my mom ran into her mom, and word is that Jasmine got a job at some high-end boutique in Manhattan. Apparently the owner thought her influencer status might draw in business."

Despite myself, I'm relieved. Sure, a part of me would have liked for her to suffer a little more, but it's true that we don't know anyone else's internal struggles, and I'm happy just to have her back out of my life. And maybe this explains that hair-touching incident I saw. But her departure doesn't change anything between me and him. "Well, the Big Apple should give her far grander things to post about than Sweetwater does."

He tips his head back in seeming agreement, then says, "Hopefully it's a new start for her."

Again, I just nod.

And as things go quiet between us and it begins snowing harder, he finally says, "I should leave you to your grave-visiting."

"I'm done," I tell him, "but it's getting pretty cold and wet out here, so I'm gonna..." I point to my car.

He nods quietly, then turns to go as well—but it's only a few seconds later that he stops and looks back at me. "Taylor, did I do something wrong?"

Caught off guard, I blink, certain I look out of sorts. "Huh?"

His demeanor has shifted and he now appears slightly angry, stone-faced. "You obviously don't want to see me anymore. I'm wondering why."

Put on the spot, I struggle to catch my breath as snow swirls around us. Although he has every right to ask, I'm viscerally whisked back to confrontations with random bullies in school. Despite that, just like when I faced Jasmine head-on last week, I steady myself and reply, "I've explained I'm super busy at the shop. Valentine's Day is only a few days away." Then I even force a smile. "Heart-shaped baked goods, you know. It's not a diner."

But my attempt at a joke falls flat, and he doesn't let me off the hook. "You sure that's the only reason?"

I take a deep breath, let it back out. And then proceed to give him a more detailed answer that's still just as empty. "Look, we're both swamped. We have very different lives. It's been nice spending time with you, but you're leaving soon, and I have cakes to make, so..."

By the time my voice trails off, a lump has risen to my throat, and I'm grateful when he begins to respond—until he confronts me with, "So we're just done? Just like that?"

I draw in another deep breath, uncomfortable. I stare at his chest, watching big snowflakes land on his coat and then melt, because I can't meet his gaze. "I'm...not sure what you want me to say."

I feel his eyes on me for a long moment until he replies, "Never mind. I get it. But just so you know, this isn't what I want."

Then when I least expect it, he steps closer, lifts one palm to my face, and kisses the opposite cheek—just before he walks away through the rows of gravestones.

I stand there in the falling snow, freezing and trying not to cry. I thought I felt that first cheek-kiss a couple of weeks ago intensely—but this one melts through me like love and passion and heartache and regret all at once.

Mom was right—I'm gonna be hurt anyway. So why am I pushing him away? As he puts more distance between us across the cemetery, I'm tempted to go after him or call his name. Tell him I'm sorry. Tell him I'm scared. Tell him I'm in too deep.

But pride won't let me.

When I knew him before, I was the girl getting laughed at, or crying in public, or whose face turned bright red from some horrible ridicule. Surely I'm that girl in *his* memory, too. And if he turned around right now, he'd see me about to cry yet again.

I just don't want to be that person anymore. I may not have much here, but at least I'll walk away with my dignity.

Despite the cold and snow, I turn back toward Dad's grave, standing there until I hear the Tahoe leave and the cemetery falls quiet again. Then I get back in my car and press the Start button.

Nothing happens. Great.

27

FEBRUARY 11

Luke

The conversation with Taylor yesterday left me deflated, so I'm nursing my wounds in the barn—currently brushing down Duchess, a little black dappled pony who loves the attention.

I've said similar things to women as what Taylor said to me in the cemetery. And what it always means is: *I'm just not that into you.*

The problem here is: She sure *seemed* into me. And just like her recent texts, the words didn't ring true.

Is that wishful thinking? The arrogant arguments of a guy who usually has women chasing him, not turning him down?

Maybe.

But the thing I loved about Taylor back in school—and

271

again recently—was her openness and authenticity. There just wasn't a fake bone in her body. Or so I thought. And I don't think she lies very well.

Unless, again, I'm deluding myself.

"Know what I like about horses?" I murmur to Duchess. "You're kind of like dogs—you don't strategize. You don't hide your feelings. You just keep things real."

In response, the pony turns her head to look at where the brush has gone still on her coat when I started talking, as if to say: *I don't mind listening, but get back to work.* It makes me laugh. A little, anyway. "Like I said, you keep it real."

I look up when Mom enters the barn in her riding gear.

"Let me finish up with Miss Duchess here," I tell her, "and then I'll grab our saddles."

Yesterday's snow, while falling briskly for a little while, didn't amount to much, and we decided it would do us both good to get out for a ride in the crisp air. I need a break from estate work, from missing the way things were with Taylor until a few days ago—from *everything*.

Well, that's a lie—not everything. I don't mind checking in every day with my Canyon Life managers, and I'm still invigorated by working on plans for the sanctuary. But the Taylor situation kind of overshadows all that right now.

Like clockwork, Mom says, "You should invite Taylor back over. I'd like to get to know her better."

I just let out a sigh and keep it short. "That's over."

I don't have to take my eyes off Duchess to sense Mom's face falling. "Oh no. Why?"

I simply shoot her a look.

Which she reads loud and clear. "Don't feel like talking about it?"

"Nope. Just feel like hanging out with the horses. And you," I remember to add.

She lets out a chuckle. "I'm grateful to be included."

"They just calm me down," I tell her of the horses as I give Duchess a little pat near her tail to shoo her gently back out into the pasture.

"You think I don't know that?" she asks without missing a beat.

It catches me off guard as I look up.

"They always have, from when you were little. Any time you got in trouble or had a disagreement with your dad, out here to the barn you came."

I try to think back. "Huh. Guess I didn't realize it went back that far. I only knew that leaving the horses when we moved was almost as hard as leaving my friends."

"Guess the horses were your friends, too," she says, leading Lady Jane from her stall. "Only in a different way."

Mom holds the palomino's bridle as I place a wool blanket on her back. "All I know is that I'm gonna miss these guys when I leave."

"They'll miss you, too," she tells me with a small smile. "You've been spoiling them in a way I can't anymore."

As I heft Lady Jane's saddle into place, I tell Mom, "Well, maybe I'll come home a little more often now. To tell you the truth, I'd like to see the farm in springtime. And summer. It's been a while." Most of my visits since Mom and Dad's return to Sweetwater have been at Thanksgiving and Christmas when nothing's green or in bloom.

That's when Mom leans around the horse's head to ask me with raised brows, "Are you sure you want to go back out west?"

I give her another pointed look. Wants are irrelevant. "I have a business to run there."

"And you have a new one to run *here*."

28

FEBRUARY 12

Luke

"Have you two been conniving with my mother?" I ask, switching my glance back and forth between TJ and Billy. We're back around the fire pit behind Billy's garage with a six-pack. Kind of like the horses, guess I find it easy to be with my old buddies, too. I have plenty of friends in Utah, but there's something about being with people who've known you forever. Even if I'm shooting them both accusing looks at the moment.

TJ appears puzzled. "What're you talking about, man?"

"She's suddenly making noise about me going back to Utah. Suggesting I should stay in Kentucky."

"Well," Billy says on a shrug, "now that you've got a big horse park to open…"

I just roll my eyes. "And two branches of another business out west."

That's when TJ narrows his gaze. "You barely mention it, though. So it must be surviving okay without you."

I slant him an irritated glance. What is it with everybody acting like I don't have an entire life somewhere else? "I've had a lot to deal with besides my business."

TJ shrugs. "Fair enough."

"And I'm lucky to have good people in place there. Lucky that even though I had to put out a few fires after I first got home, since then it's been problem-free."

"There ya go," he replies on a grin, lightly crushing a beer can in his fist. "You can move back to Sweetwater where you belong."

I ignore that, not only because I'm annoyed by it, but because something catches my eye behind Billy. A dark red RAV4 I normally wouldn't notice—except for the little red fabric heart hanging from the rearview mirror. It saw it every time Taylor met me someplace. "Is that Taylor's car?"

Billy glances over his shoulder. "Oh. Yeah. Had to tow it from the cemetery the other day. Alternator went out on her with no warning. Waiting for a part—hopefully tomorrow."

I let my eyes bolt open wide, realizing it must have been right after our conversation there. "Was she okay? Did she have to wait in the cold very long?"

Billy's look suggests I'm overreacting. Maybe I am, but I don't like thinking of her being stranded. "Relax, bud—I was there with the tow truck fifteen minutes after she called."

I nod, relieved, but also aware that she didn't choose to call *me*, even though I'd just left and was surely a lot closer than Billy.

I shake off that discouraging thought, though, as something else hits me. "Damn—I was supposed to let you know you won a cake from the bake shop."

My old friend makes a celebratory fist, pulling it back toward him with a, "Cha-ching! About time, too. Been dropping my card in that box for years." Then he leans slightly forward across the fire from me, until I realize he's staring me down. "Why do you look so depressed, man? Is it about your dad?"

I take a deep breath, blow it back out. Apparently I don't possess a poker face. But no reason not to be honest. "Nah," I say. "It's…Taylor."

"Huh?" Billy mutters.

"Taylor Mulvaney?" TJ asks—as if we all know anyone else named Taylor.

Then Billy casts me a sly grin. "I wondered what was going on when you announced the horse park was her idea."

"The horse park was her idea?" TJ echoes. Despite getting permission for me to use the gym, he wasn't at that second meeting and appears completely confused.

"Yes, it was her idea. And we've seen each other some since I got home. Not a lot," I go on, "because we've both been busy. But the times we got together were…really good."

Billy keeps grinning at me, and TJ looks like a guy trying to wrap his head around a shocking new concept.

I decide to take mercy on him and provide a little more background. "I've been into her since high school."

"You have?" TJ just gapes at me, still sounding completely in the dark.

"She stood me up at the sweetheart dance when we were seniors, and that's how I ended up with Jasmine that night."

At this, TJ's jaw drops. "Well, *this* is news. And you think you know somebody." He rolls his eyes.

And I can't help it—I laugh. "You sound just like an adolescent girl, Teej." But that quickly, my laughter is long gone. "When she didn't show, I was embarrassed, and too immature, I guess, to fill you guys in."

"Well, let's get back to the present," Billy says, looking keenly interested in the subject. "You seeing her now?"

"No," I correct him. "I *was*. That's why I look depressed, remember? Keep up."

"Details," TJ demands.

I release a sigh and let my gaze land in the crackling flames as I think it through. "Things were going great. Great conversation. Great everything. Even though it was fast, I thought we were on the verge of taking it further, when—*boom*, she suddenly wants nothing to do with me. I asked if I did something wrong and she said no. So I have no idea why things changed."

Across the fire, Billy strokes his chin like a detective in thought—then offers up, "If you ask me, Taylor doesn't seem like a woman to be into something casual."

"Who said I wanted something casual?" I counter.

"Dude," TJ injects, "you live a million miles away. She has a business here; you have a business *there*. It probably seemed like a non-starter when she stopped and thought about it. What else could it be?"

Okay, is he actually making sense here? I can't decide, a little befuddled. "Well, yeah, but...I mean...I never said..."

"Maybe that's the problem," TJ informs me. "You never said...whatever she might have needed to hear."

Billy slants me an accusing glance. "The trouble with this guy, Teej, is that he's had it too easy with girls. Mr. Good-Looking Romeo over here has never had to work for it—they just flock to him."

"And now he's finding out the hard way that sometimes you have to *think*." TJ concludes by actually pointing at his head like I'm some kind of numbskull.

I lower my chin to ask, "Are you guys saying I'm an idiot?"

Billy gives his head a pointed tilt. "Like I said, I don't know Taylor well, but...it's safe to say she's not like other girls you've dated."

"Hey, I've been gone a long time—you have no idea who I've dated."

My friends just look at each other. "Sure we do," TJ replies. "Super confident, super gorgeous girls who know what they want and probably aren't afraid to chase after it."

Upon thinking that through for a minute, I'm a big enough man to confess, "Okay. Guilty as charged."

"And that's not Taylor Mulvaney," Billy points out.

"Nope," TJ agrees.

I glance suspiciously back and forth between them. "Since when do you guys know Taylor so well?"

They both go wide-eyed, like I'm a jealous boyfriend who needs to check himself. Maybe I do. My head's all over the place.

"Bruh, I just fix her car and buy the occasional snack from her. Settle down."

But then I narrow in on TJ. "What about *you*?"

He throws up his hands in innocence. "Hey, I'm just a regular in the bake shop. The lady makes a mean cookie, after all. And I gotta see my girl, Mags. But you can relax because that's as far as it goes, Romeo." Then he cocks me a sideways glance. "And you could do worse. Too bad you messed up."

I blow out another breath, analyzing the situation. "So... what you're saying is, she thinks I'm leaving, and she thinks I'm not in this in any real way?"

"Probably," Billy replies.

TJ just shrugs, asking, "And aren't you? Leaving?"

"Well, yeah. But..."

"But what?"

That's when it hits me. The last time things felt normal between Taylor and me, she asked me how running the park "would work" and I cheerfully told her I'd be back a few times a year. And the truth is—with so much going on the past six weeks, every bit of it unexpected and jarring, I just wasn't thinking that far ahead. I guess I assumed that if our relationship progressed, we'd cross that bridge when we came to it, but...I sure never said it. I never said *anything*.

"Okay, in fairness to me, though," I tell them, puzzling through it out loud now, "this thing between us was really new, so I didn't think we were at a point where I needed to... declare my feelings or talk about the future." I stop, sigh. "But by the same token, maybe I needed to...remember the girl I was dealing with."

That, like TJ said, her business that ties her to this town.

That I'm not sure she's navigated a lot of relationships. And that, yeah, she doesn't seem like a woman who'd be into a casual fling. All of that should have been obvious to me. But I missed every bit of it, too caught up in other things.

"In a way," I go on, pausing to shake my head, "this is just like high school all over again. I didn't make sure she knew I was really *in* this. And I've just realized...I am."

And maybe that won't make a difference. But I at least have to let her know.

I can't fix my past mistakes. I can't fix *anything* about the past. But there's one night I can try to re-do to give us both a new, better memory.

29

FEBRUARY 13

Luke

As I pull Dad's SUV to one of the curbside spots lining Main Street, it's more crowded than usual, and a glance at the Sweetheart Bake Shop tells me the place is hopping. Which makes sense—it's the day before Valentine's Day and, as she's made very clear to me, this is her busy time.

Well, it doesn't matter whether or not I see her today—either way, I'm just here to drop the little envelope in my pocket into the heart-shaped box on the counter.

Even so, as I push through the door, my heart pounds like a drum against my chest. *Damn, you've got it bad for this girl.* I'm only glad I figured it out, with a little help from my friends, in time to try to do something about it.

Glancing around the diner—or, wait, bake shop—I see people waiting to place or collect orders, Geneva boxing up a heart-shaped cherry pie, Kyra ringing out customers, and a couple of booths taken by patrons snacking on cupcakes or cookies. But no Taylor. She must be in the back, baking.

The letdown washes through me in a wave that nearly knocks me off balance. I guess I really *did* want to see her, want to make eye contact across the shop, want her to spot me putting something in the box. Again, I've got it bad for Taylor Mulvaney.

But this is okay. I knew she might be busy in the kitchen. So I proceed with the plan.

When an older woman leaves the counter, pink box in hand, I step up. Kyra has already glanced toward Geneva to say, "I see Mrs. Brown parking, here for the Girl Scout troop cupcakes. I'll help you as soon as I get a minute."

I use the time to insert my small envelope into the box, flashing back to valentines I slid through the same slot years ago. Funny, I'd thought those days were long over.

That's when Kyra turns to me to say, "How can I help— oh, it's you. Hi."

Keeping my voice low, I ask, "Can you do me a favor, like once before? Can you make sure Taylor looks inside this box by tomorrow."

"Oh. *Absolutely*," Kyra replies, her eyes suggesting she's grasped that something romantic's afoot.

"Promise me you won't forget," I insist. "It's important."

She flashes a conspiratorial grin to say, "No worries—you can count on me."

Taylor

"Hey, Taylor!"

I lift my head from where I'm rolling out peanut butter cookie dough to meet Kyra's gaze in the pass-through window. "Yep?"

"Be sure to look in your heart box later, okay?"

This seems out of the blue. "All right. What's in there?"

"I don't know. But just look inside."

I shrug. "Okay, sure." *Whatever that's about.*

"Hey, Taylor." This time it's Geneva through the window.

I shift my gaze to her. "Yeah?"

"We're getting short on peanut butter cookies."

I answer with a quick nod. "Working on that now. Anything else running low?"

"Cupcakes are flying off the shelves," she tells me.

I nod again and blow out a tired breath. "I've got six dozen coming out of the oven in..." I glance at the timer. "Two minutes. If you get a break, you can frost them. If not, I'll get to them ASAP."

30

FEBRUARY 14

Taylor

It's been a long few days in more ways than one. We've stayed busy at the bake shop, I don't have my car but do have a new alternator to pay Finch Auto Repair for whenever it comes in, and...every time I think of Luke—which is often—I almost can't breathe. But I try to tell myself: *If it's this bad already, imagine if things had gotten more serious and* then *he was suddenly out of your life.*

On the upside: I'm alone with Maggie in the shop, having just sent Geneva and Kyra home for a much-deserved rest. It's after seven, and I'm still working—mixing up a batch of icing—but we haven't had any customers since five and soon I'll close up and head home myself, another Valentine's Day in the books.

Just then, the front door opens and in walks Billy Finch.

I let my eyes bolt open wide. "Please tell me you're here because my car's ready," I say through the interior window.

He gives his head an I'm-about-to-disappoint-you tilt. "Sorry, Taylor. Still waiting on that part, but when I called earlier, the guy promised I'll *really* have it tomorrow." Then he smiles. "I'm here for my free cake." His smile fades, though, as he inspects the display cabinet. "If you have any left."

I set aside my work and walk around to take a glance myself. When a lock of hair that's escaped my ponytail blocks my vision, I shove it behind one ear. "We've got a chocolate one with chocolate ganache and a strawberry one with whipped buttercream frosting. If neither of those speak to you, let me know what you'd like and I'll make it tomorrow."

He shrugs. "I'll take the strawberry. Jessie Ann likes strawberry."

Jessie Ann is Billy's longtime girlfriend and I'm guessing he's forgotten to get her anything for Valentine's Day and has just found out the florist outside town is out of flowers, which my *last* male customer shared with me. When a guy shows up this late on February fourteenth, that's usually the case.

As I box up the cake, I inform him, "If you need a card, the drugstore's still open."

His alarmed expression tells me he forgot that, too. "You're a lifesaver, Taylor."

It's been an exhausting couple of days, no longer with mail order fulfillment but instead walk-in business, and my brain is fried—but I guess some of the circuits are still connecting.

As I hand him a pretty pink box, I say, "Happy Valentine's Day, Billy." That's what we do here on February fourteenth. We wish every customer a happy heart-filled holiday. Even if we're not really feeling happy ourselves—and I'm not, but I think I fake it pretty well.

"Happy Valentine's Day, Taylor."

When he's gone, I glance down at my faithful companion, Maggie, whose tongue lolls from one side of her mouth. "And happy Valentine's Day to you, too, Mags," I say softly. "Looks like it's just me and you, as usual. What do you say I lock up and we head home? There's a frozen lasagna dinner with my name on it, and maybe I'll treat us both to a cupcake. We deserve it, right?"

As I turn back to the counter, a blob of wet icing drops right on to the valentine box in front of me, and I realize instantly that it came from my hair. "Oh my God," I mutter, "how long has *that* been there?" Well, not very, since it didn't have time to dry—it must be from the batch I was mixing when Billy came in. And—crud—it might leave a stain on the box. Which is not the end of the world because I can always paint it again, but...

That's when I realize the icing blob has spread into the loose shape of a heart. One side is bigger than the other, but it's still a heart.

And then I gasp. Kyra reminded me twice today to look in the box, but I was so busy each time that it went in one ear and out the other. I totally forgot, thinking in the moment that maybe she'd put a valentine inside for me.

But when I see a heart that way, it's usually more important than, say, a card from a friend. "What now, Dad?" I whisper. Then I unlatch the lid and pull it off.

On top of the usual business cards lies a small red envelope with my name neatly printed on it. Ah, maybe it *is* just a card from Kyra. Sweet of her.

Slipping my finger inside the sealed flap, I open it up and pull out an old-fashioned valentine like we used to give each other in school. Overtop a cartoonish red pony, it says: *Stop horsing around and be my valentine.*

I smile, then flip it over—and get the shock of my life. Or —well—the *second* shock of my life that's come from this box.

It's not from Kyra.

I still recognize Luke's handwriting from valentines and heart wishes long ago, even before seeing his name. But it's not just his name he's written.

Meet me in the school gym on Valentine's Day at 7:15 PM. Word of the day: Dance. You still owe me one.

What? My tired mind tries to process the note. Luke wants me to be his valentine and he's asked me with a horse, which is adorable. And he wants me to meet him for a dance? At the school? That part hardly makes sense.

And didn't I just push him away? Don't I keep telling myself it's for the best? So why is my heart beating so fast right now? Why is my first impulse to fly to where he is and let myself be swept up in his strong arms? Maybe I've never forgotten that fantasy I once concocted about walking into that gym in a gorgeous dress.

Well, *that's* an absolute impossibility. I look down at the dirty apron I'm wearing over an also-dirty *Sweetheart Bake Shop (Not a Diner!)* T-shirt, then remember my hair's in a messy ponytail and also has icing in it. After which I glance up at the old diner clock still on the wall above the door to see it's 7:20.

7:20*!*

I'm late already—but at least it didn't take me four years to find *this* invitation.

"Mags, we've got to go! Fast!"

Throwing my apron off over my head, I rush to lock the front door, scoop up my dog in my arms, grab my purse, and rush out the back, locking that door, too. All the while I'm remembering there's a huge batch of icing I didn't put in the fridge, but I have to let it go.

Only—my parking spot out back is empty! Where's my car?

Oh no. It's at Billy's. I was planning to walk home. But it's a lot farther to the school than my house.

What to do? I stand there frozen—because I forgot my coat—with an armful of poodle and no idea how I'm going to get where I need to go.

"Wait," I say to Maggie. "I can text him. I can text him and tell him I'll be on my way as soon as I figure out how."

It's not easy to finagle my phone from my purse with a dog in my arms, but I manage it. Only to find it won't come on. Really? I was so busy I forgot to charge it? That *never* happens. But it just did.

In pure desperation, I sprint up the alley beside my shop and emerge onto Main Street to find lights still on in the drugstore. I run with Maggie in that direction and, through the window, spot Jeff and Billy chatting. I burst through the door like a madwoman. "I need a ride!"

They both turn toward me, jaws dropping.

"Huh?" Billy asks.

As Jeff asks with grave concern, "Taylor, are you okay?"

"I need a ride! Now! It's an emergency!"

"Are you hurt?" Jeff asks, eyes filled with worry.

"No—I just need a ride! Billy, give me a ride!"

Billy looks discombobulated, fumbling frantically with his wallet. "I need to pay for my card."

"He'll pay you later, Jeff," I say through clenched teeth. "C'mon, let's go! It's urgent!"

"All right, all right—I'm coming. Calm down. I don't want to damage my cake."

He's still not moving fast enough for me, but once we're in his pickup, me with a dog in my lap, he asks cautiously, "Okay, where are we going? The hospital? An all-night vet?"

"No, the high school," I inform him.

He looks across the truck cab at me, clearly even more perplexed than before. "The high school?"

"Yes! Don't just sit there—drive!"

As the truck pulls away from the curb, Billy begins to look frightened, like maybe he's in the company of someone who should instead be driven to a psychiatric ward. The truck is moving now, but Billy says very calmly to me, "Taylor, there are no events at the high school tonight. Nobody will be there. Do you need me to call your mom?"

I turn my frantic gaze on him, feeling as crazed at this point as I probably seem. I guess his concern makes sense—I haven't explained very well, or...at all. Now I attempt to speak calmly. "Luke is there, waiting for me. He left me a valentine, but I didn't find it until just now. I'm already late, and if I don't get there quickly, he'll think I'm standing him up again."

"Oh," he says, taking all this in. And then he *really* seems to get it. "*Ohhh*. Why didn't ya say so?" After which he floors it.

Luke

Here I stand in the school gym, holding another dozen red roses, alone.

It's worse this time in a way. I made a grand gesture. I got TJ to let me into our old school one more time and I actually tried to recreate the sweetheart dance Taylor and I never got to share.

And I took it for granted that everything Billy and TJ said the other night accurately explained her pulling back and that this would fix things. Or that—hell—she'd at least be curious enough to check it out. Or kind enough not to leave me hanging in rejected humiliation.

Damn, even now, the rejection stings.

It's almost 7:45. It's ridiculous I've waited *this* long. I mean, when will I get the message? *Wake up, Montgomery. She's not coming. She's doesn't love you.*

I guess I deserve this. It's the first time I've really cared about someone who didn't return my feelings. And worse still, I'm pretty sure I've fallen in love with her. It seems crazy after only being home a little more than a month, but this goes back further. When you have history with someone, everything in the present means more.

Or at least it did to me.

I think it's time for this disillusioned Romeo to just slink on back to the farm. Then get back to the things I still need to accomplish before leaving Sweetwater, since I'm suddenly eager to hightail it back to Utah where I won't have to worry about running into the girl who's broken my heart—again.

Taylor

It's surreal to lug my dog into the school gym and find the stage at the far end dimly lit, hung with fairy lights and foil hearts. Luke Montgomery stands upon it wearing a dark suit and red tie, holding a dozen roses limp at his side, looking as handsome as I've ever seen him. The sight halts me in place.

When our gazes connect across the distance, he lifts the bouquet back up, and his voice comes soft but deep. "If it's not Taylor Mulvaney, keeper of the heart wishes."

I carry Maggie closer. "I didn't think they still had the sweetheart dance here," is all I can think of to say.

"This is just for us," he informs me. "For that dance we never got to have."

Standing below the stage now, peering up at him, I shake my head and say, "Look at me. I'm a mess. And I had to bring Mags because there was no time to take her home. If I'd found your note sooner, I would be in a pretty dress right now, looking as amazing as you do." Then I stop, shake my head. "Or, well, maybe not, actually, because you look perfect and..." I stop talking because I've just accidentally blurted out that he's perfect. Because he is.

"Like I said once before, you're a *gorgeous* mess," he tells me. "I promise, you look perfect to me, too, exactly the way you are."

Once upon a time, I fantasized about walking into this gym looking beautiful, trying to measure up to the kind of girls I thought Luke liked—but in this moment, I feel total acceptance from the handsome man before me, just as I am.

Now that man descends the steps to one side of the stage to meet me, handing me the roses as he takes the fluffy dog from my arms and lowers her to the floor. Which I guess is okay, because where is she gonna go? "I'm right here, Mags," I murmur to let her hear my voice.

"Don't worry, Maggie," Luke says. "She's not going anywhere. She's finally where she's supposed to be—even if she's a little late." Then he meets my gaze. "I was afraid you weren't coming."

"I didn't check the box—we've been swamped."

"Maybe it was a bad idea to rely on the box again, but...it just felt right."

"It *was* right," I assure him. "But I also don't have transportation right now—my car's in the shop."

His eyes bolt wide. "Oh, damn—I actually knew that, but I was so nervous I totally forgot."

She appears stunned. "*You* were nervous?"

He nods like that should make sense to me. "When I make a big play for the woman who keeps pushing me away because, despite all the very clear messages she's sending, I'm still not ready to give up on her...yeah, that makes me nervous."

The words, along with the vulnerability shining through his eyes, serve to remind me how I once accidentally stood him up, and how his father didn't come to his games, and how it all left him feeling rejected. I hate that he's ever had to feel that way. "Please know I'll always show up for you," I tell him. "Even if I have..." I look down, taking myself in. "...Stains on my shirt and icing in my hair."

But he just smiles and says, "Come with me."

Taking my hand, he leads me up the steps and onto the stage. Once there, he extracts the bouquet from my arms and lowers it to a small table where a portable speaker resides, then pulls out his phone and hits a few buttons. Music emerges from the speaker— "Lady in Red" by Chris de Burgh begins to play.

Luke holds out his hand to ask, "May I have this dance?"

"You remembered?" I whisper about the song. "All these years?"

"I couldn't forget anything about the girl I always should have been dancing with."

And then that's what we do—we dance. We don't talk. We just sway to the same song that was so meaningful to my parents, and I let it become an even bigger part of me now. It's about a man taking in the beauty of the woman he's with, and as Luke gazes down at me while we move together, his affection is undeniable—even with the icing, even with the stains. His eyes make me feel more beautiful than I knew I could.

When his mouth meets mine, I melt into him, forgetting

everything that's led up to this, sinking completely into the moment. I smell things like leather and sugar and old bleachers. I get lost in the song and the warmth of his body pressed against me. I was a fool to push him away. No matter what the future holds, or doesn't, this moment alone is worth any risk.

After we break from kissing, he whispers, his face near mine, "You always taste as sweet as the things you bake."

And I reply with what's in my heart, unedited, unfiltered. "I'm going to miss you so, so much when you leave, Luke. That's why I pushed you away. I'm sorry. I should have been honest. It was all because I'm going to miss you."

"No, Taylor," he says, "you're not."

I pull back to look up at him, confused, as the song comes to an end and the gym falls silent once more. My voice echoes as I ask, "What do you mean?"

"I've been doing a lot of thinking," he begins. "About things *I'd* miss here if I leave again. The horses. My mom. My old buddies. The farm. The hot girl at the bake shop." Then he grins down at me. "Mainly the last one, though."

Hot. No one has ever called me hot in my life. But Luke Montgomery just did. And I can barely process what he's just said to me—the actual important part—only then I finally do. "But...your business," I say. "And you *love* Utah."

"Yeah, I do," he concedes. "But there's a lot to love here, too. I just never noticed it when I was a kid. Well, wait." He lowers his gaze, bringing our faces closer. "I noticed *one* thing to love then—you. But I didn't think you noticed back. Anyway, maybe it's time for a new chapter. I've loved my life out west. Now I'm gonna love my life back home."

Okay, maybe I'm still having trouble computing things here, but... "Did you just say you...love me?"

His eyebrows shoot up playfully, like maybe he didn't completely mean for that to come out. "Yeah, guess I did. Too fast?"

"No," I assure him, peering up into that blue gaze.

Then he laughs. "Good. Because I *do* love you, Taylor. It started way back when. And maybe that was only a crush, an infatuation. But getting to know you again now...you've stolen my heart all over again. I'm sorry if it took a little while to realize what you needed from me, and that I want to stay."

I shrug, still in his warm embrace. "Well, a month," I murmur, happy to absolve him. "That's reasonable."

And that's when I see hearts all around us. They're not like usual—not something in nature or in fabric or on a wall, not something you can touch. They're pale and translucent, floating all around us. And maybe they're only in my head. Or maybe they're a gift from my father in one of the best moments of my life.

I gaze up at Luke and ask, "Would you kiss me again?"

He grins down at me. "That's something you never have to ask for. In fact, get ready, because you're gonna get kissed so much you're gonna get tired of it."

"Not possible," I tell him.

"Well, let's give it a try."

Epilogue
One Year Later

Taylor

I stand before a full-length mirror in the largest suite of the Sweetwater Inn, studying my reflection. I'm wearing my wedding gown. And there's no icing or flour in my hair today.

Caroline and Mom helped me into my dress a little while ago, and now they're in the next room getting ready themselves, and putting Maggie in the most adorable little red heart-laden doggie dress ever. I asked to have a few minutes alone, just to soak in the moment.

It's amazing how much has happened since Luke and I finally got to share that dance.

Last August, the Sweetheart Horse Park and Sanctuary opened for business. We now have seventeen horses on-site, and even in winter, business has stayed brisk.

Luke's mom moved into the guesthouse, insisting she

wanted a smaller place, and she's thrown herself into admin work for the sanctuary, managing the gift shop as well.

In June, Sweetwater will host the First Annual Hearts and Horses Festival, with a parade and events all over town, capped at the end with the dedication of a plaque and memorial garden honoring Dr. Montgomery.

As hoped, Sweetwater's Main Street is suddenly showing new signs of life. In addition to business picking up for Sweet Caroline's and the drugstore, a pizza place is set to open soon and there's talk of an antique shop moving in.

Meanwhile, Jasmine seems to be rebounding wildly in Manhattan, and if not enough miracles have occurred already, a few months ago when she was home for Thanksgiving, she posted a picture of one of my heart-shaped drizzle cakes to her now-back-up-to-four-million-plus followers, linking to the shop with the caption: *A whole shop full of sweet hearts.* Long story short, after some hectic days during December, I've now hired two new full-time employees.

When I hear my phone buzz across the room, I leave the mirror and take a seat in a chair next to a big picture window looking out on the gently flowing Ohio River in the wintry dusk. I snatch it up to see a text from my man.

Hi, keeper of my heart. He used to call me the "keeper of the heart wishes," but it's evolved.

I type back, *See you at the altar, cowboy?* Truly, the hat has grown on me.

He answers with: *Wild horses couldn't drag me away.*

A rocky start in life doesn't mean it always has to stay that way, and my heart is fuller than it's ever been as I pick up one of our heart-shaped wedding invitations from the table next to me.

Taylor and Luke invite you share in their joy as they exchange vows on

February 14, 7:00 PM
at the
Sweetwater Inn
873 Main Street
Sweetwater, KY

Wear pink or red, and come ready to slow dance to romantic songs, eat heart-shaped wedding cake from the Sweetheart Bake Shop, and drop your Valentine's Day wishes for the happy couple in the heart-shaped box that brought them together over and over—until they realized it was meant to be, forever.

Also by Toni Blake

The Box Books

The Wedding Box

The Christmas Box

The Valentine Box

The Summer Island trilogy

The One Who Stays

The Giving Heart

The Love We Keep

The Rose Brothers trilogy

Brushstrokes

Mistletoe

Heartstrings

The Coral Cove trilogy

All I Want is You

Love Me if You Dare

Take Me All the Way

The Destiny Series

One Reckless Summer

Sugar Creek

Whisper Falls

Holly Lane

Willow Springs

Half Moon Hill

Christmas in Destiny

Return to Destiny

Standalone Novels

Wildest Dreams

The Red Diary

Letters to a Secret Lover

Tempt Me Tonight

Swept Away

The Mandy Project

The Perfect Mistake

The Weekend Wife

The Bewitching Hour

The Guy Next Door

The Cinderella Scheme

About the Author

Toni Blake's love of writing began when she won an essay contest in the fifth grade. Soon after, she penned her first novel, nineteen notebook pages long. Since then, Toni has become a RITA™-nominated author of over thirty contemporary romance novels, her books have received the National Readers' Choice Award and Bookseller's Best Award, and her work has been excerpted in *Cosmo*. Toni lives in the Midwest and enjoys traveling, crafts, and spending time outdoors.

www.toniblake.com